LIBERATOR

Stefanie Dawn

Liberator
Elements of Abduction
Book 4

Stefanie Dawn

This book is a work of fiction. Any references to real events, real people, and real places are used fictitiously. Other names, characters, places and incidents are products of the Author's imagination and any resemblance to persons, living or dead, actual events, organizations or places is entirely coincidental.

All rights are reserved. This book is intended for the purchaser of this book ONLY. No part of this book may be reproduced or transmitted in any form or by any means, graphic, electronic, or mechanical, including photocopying, recording, taping, or by any information storage retrieval system, without the express written permission of the Author. All songs, song titles and lyrics contained in this book are the property of the respective songwriters and copyright holders.

Disclaimer: The material in this book contains graphic language and sexual content and is intended for mature audiences, ages 18 and older.

ISBN: 978-1763870512

Editing and Proofing by Swish Design & Editing
Book Design by Swish Design & Editing
Cover Design by Eric at
The Book Brander
Published by Angels and Fire Books
Cover Image Copyright 2024

First Edition
Copyright © 2024 Angels and Fire Books
All Rights Reserved

DEDICATION

For Ashleigh.
Look, a book dedication!
Just for you!

LIBERATOR

CHAPTER

I

MISHA

The aliens who abducted me from my home and taken me far from Earth—shoved me unceremoniously into an escape pod of some sort. Before I could even react, I was shot out of their ship and drifted down until I landed on the alien planet below. I lost track of the other pods that carried the girls I'd been taken with as mine spun, and I barely kept the contents of my stomach where they should be as the world blurred through the small viewing window. It leveled out only when what I assumed was a parachute of some sort slowed my descent.

Gripping my chest, I tried to ease my panic and

took as many mental notes of the terrain before me as I could as I was eased to the surface. I was headed toward the ocean—a deep, dirty gray color—and huge waves crashed over the sandy gray shore.

Please don't let me land in the water.

I could swim, but those waves looked dangerous and unpredictable, and I was weak from only having eaten basic white nutrient bars for weeks. I caught a glimpse of what could have been a village over a tree line, and when I went to stand in my pod to get a better look, I hit my head on the harsh interior. Cursing, I pushed my fingers through my curly hair and rubbed at the sore spot.

That wasn't a trick of my eye. I *definitely* saw a village or at least a potentially populated area over those trees.

As I continued to fall, the village seemed farther and farther away, and I kept my eyes glued to the spot where I'd seen it, desperate not to lose my bearings so I could head for it as soon as I landed.

Hopefully, whoever was there could help, and maybe they even knew *why* we'd been taken and then simply tossed from the ship like garbage.

They'd experimented on us onboard the ship, each time stopping just short of anything too intrusive. They'd do enough to make my heart rate race, squeeze my eyes shut, and hope what I *thought* was about to happen wasn't going to happen—then they'd stop.

They'd probed my mouth, ears, and belly button.

They'd poked and prodded me enough to make me bruise.

Then, right before we'd been ejected from the ship, they'd come at me with what looked like a giant gun filled with equally giant sperm, but then stopped before they'd touched me with it.

Evidently, we weren't what they wanted. It felt like a blessing and a damn miracle.

But now I was faced with an entire world—pun not intended—of new problems. This was beyond being in a strange country and not sharing a common language. I had no idea what would and wouldn't be food here, what the customs were, or what sort of wildlife hid in those woods and the water. The idea aliens existed had only ever been a fun thing to think about, but now I'd seen things I'd never even imagined, and literally *anything* could be waiting for me on the surface.

The pod hit the ground with a soft thud and immediately rolled onto its side when there was no traction on the sand. My shoulder collided with the side of the pod, and I groaned as the door slid open and disappeared into the side of the pod as if it was never there.

The scent of the ocean hit me first—strong and more than salty. It smelled like a dulled-down health-food store with too many scents all piled one on top of the other, and the smell increased in strength with each wave that crashed over itself. It wasn't entirely unpleasant but a hefty reminder this wasn't Earth.

As if I needed another reminder.

I crawled out of the pod, feeling a bit foolish in my pajamas with little horses on them—the sort of pajamas I thought were cute but didn't think anyone else would ever see. They were ripped and partially shredded, I had no shoes, and I was caked in weeks of my own grime and sweat.

Sexy.

It was only me and my horsey-pajamas against a new world of possible dangers, and I had only one thought on my mind.

Get help.

And help was in the form of whatever lived in that village. I didn't waste a moment and immediately began walking across the smooth sand toward the trees, past which I'd seen the village. All I needed to do was follow parallel to the water. The beach had ended when rocks had protruded from the land, atop which were the trees.

And no matter how much doubt crept into my mind, I kept reminding myself I was *certain* the village I'd seen was just beyond those trees.

Where the sand met the trees had seemed so close when I was in the pod, and I tried to settle the gurgling of my nervous stomach by simply putting one foot in front of the other. I could see a blur of something in the distance, and I told myself with as much conviction as I could manage that it was the trees I sought.

The bright orange sun pounded against my back, and the shore appeared never-ending. It felt like hours before the trees seemed closer, sitting atop a small rocky outcrop where the sand morphed into the woodlands. The area looked lush and green, and as silly as it was, I found that comforting.

Green was familiar, green was nice, and reminded me of the wooded area surrounding my riding school, where I took children on trail rides and went out alone to clear my mind.

What I wouldn't give to have Charlie, the horse I'd had since I was fourteen years old, with me. But I had to suffice with the images on my clothes and rubbed my hand absentmindedly over the print on the fabric—little gray horses like Charlie.

I kept walking.

Closer to the rocks, my thirst became a problem I could no longer ignore. Stopping, I turned and faced the ocean. The ocean back home was too salty to drink, but was this? It *majorly* sucked that I had only one way of knowing, and that was risky.

Try the water.

My dry lips smacked together as I approached the shore and stood uneasily at the water's edge. I glanced around as if help would suddenly manifest and tell me what to do. But the beach was as deserted as it had been all day, and when squinting, I couldn't even see my pod in the distance anymore.

Crouching by the edge of the ocean, I stuck my finger in the water, lifted it to my mouth, and rubbed the warm liquid against my lips. Letting my tongue dart out, I tentatively tasted it.

It tasted like it smelled—not salty, but minerally like when you open a jar of vitamins and get that whiff of chemically-produced supplements.

And I didn't immediately die or shit my pants so that was a bonus.

Kneeling, I scooped a small amount of the water into my palms, gently sipped at it, and waited for something bad to happen.

Although a small voice in my head reminded me, *If there are weird alien microbes or bacteria in the water, I might not know straightaway, and could die hours later.*

"Thanks, brain, that's really helpful." I sighed. If that were the case, I'd have no chance on this planet regardless, so, "Bottoms up," I muttered and downed the rest of the water in my hands before quickly scooping up another handful and repeating until my thirst was quenched, and I felt more human.

Standing, I stretched my arms above my head before shaking them out and turned to resume my

journey to the village.
    Toward help.

SAHCOR

The image of the unit descending from the sky was blurred and rippled as I watched from under the ocean's surface. The sun played patterns on the top of the water, light glinting off the waves and the unit itself, and it took me a moment to realize what I was looking at.

It had been so long.

Bursting above the surface, I treaded water and watched the unit descend to the beach. Whoever was in that unit was my responsibility—they had landed closest to my territory, and so it was my job to rescue them.

It seemed the Ghaal were still bringing species here, kidnapped illegally from their home planets by pirates desperate enough for supplies to do the Ghaal's bidding, and dropped here to be experimented on. To find out if they were compatible to breed with the Ghaal to save their dying species.

My brothers and I did our best to get to the units before the Ghaal did and steer the occupants away from the colony, warning them of the danger there.

I'd lost sight of the unit as it landed, but the beach was mostly clear of trees or rocks, so finding it would be easy enough. Of course, it would have to land when I was so far out into the ocean. I didn't come out this far too often—only when I really needed to feel free.

And because the hacku fish never came closer to the shore, if I timed it right and got out here when the sun was high, they'd be closer to the surface—a delicious treat but an effort to hunt. They were fast, and even with my webbed toes and fingers, I could only maintain that speed for a short period under water.

I was not originally a water being. Being a Synth—a lab-created species—my brothers and I were designed to adapt to our environment. My station near the ocean molded me over time until I could blend in and thrive here. I often wondered what my brothers looked like—Ilk in the mountains, Eldich in the sandy woodlands, Ryth in the river system—and how much their environments had changed them.

Would I even recognize them anymore after all these years?

Our eyes were a dead giveaway—a bright green that never changed regardless of the adaptation.

I missed my brothers.

I wasn't a leader like Ilk, a joker like Vitri, and perhaps not even a protector like Lanir. Although the desire to protect ran thick within our genes, much as the desire to breed was basically what drove us to live. I preferred to sit back and observe—listen to their conversations and interactions and simply be a part of them, a part of the only family I'd ever known.

We weren't brothers by blood, each formed with a random assortment of lab-created and Ghaal DNA—a dying scientist's last gift to the dwindling Ghaal population. But seeing my brothers as family made it easier when we were tortured together and encouraged to change genders to breed—a transformation that was painful and we tried to prevent.

To save the population of a species that didn't deserve to live.

And why we escaped.

I had volunteered to be stationed closest to the colony. Lanir would tear them apart if he were too close, but he also refused to be the farthest away, a station that Ryth took. I encouraged Vitri to take the forest as I wanted to protect him. Despite everything we went through, he had an innocence about him that needed to be protected and preserved.

But to business now—find the pod and save the being inside from getting too close to the Ghaal.

Taking a deep breath—while I had gills, breathing above the surface was easier and gave me more strength—I dived under the water and headed toward the shore.

She was beautiful.

I don't know why I should be so taken aback that the kidnapped species be female—they were what the Ghaal needed to breed. However, gender was not always so black and white, especially between planets and galaxies.

But *she* was everything feminine that stirred up desire in me.

All the parts of my DNA I thought would have become dormant after all this time without a female to desire, care for, and breed sprung to life with such sudden vitality I sunk back under the surface of the churning ocean to distract myself.

And to let loose the groan that arose without startling her when my cock hardened.

She hadn't seen me. I'd found her walking along the shore, the unit she came in nowhere to be seen. She must have been walking for some time.

And she was headed straight toward the Ghaal colony.

I had no time to waste. I needed to stop her and keep her safe, but my erection was painful and throbbing, and I groaned again.

It seemed my ability to adapt didn't overrun the original design of my DNA—to breed.

To *fuck.*

Only it laid dormant in my system, and quiet enough, I assumed it was no longer there. Admittedly, I'd become a shell of who I used to be, taking each day one at a time, alive but not living.

But this is the life we chose to keep innocents from becoming Ghaal victims. It was honorable and right, and I didn't regret it.

Kicking my feet, I breached the water's surface just enough that my eyes were above it, and my deep-purple, shoulder-length hair—a remnant from my original form—spread out across the water around me.

The sunlight reflected off her hair, throwing shades of deep red amongst the dark curls. I slowly moved forward through the water, needing to get closer. I told myself it was because I needed to save her, which wasn't a lie, but the complete truth was since I laid eyes on her, I'd been unable to get the image of her underneath me and taking my cock from my mind.

No other abducted species had drawn this reaction from me.

Closer...

She stopped walking, staring out across the water, and a deep furrow settled between her brows before her eyes went wide.

No. Not staring across the water.

Staring at *me.*

Unwilling to appear as though I was spying on her, I planted my feet on the ocean's sandy floor and stood, the water splashing around my chest as I came to my full height.

She took a step away from me.

I held out my hand in what I hoped was a calming gesture. "Don't be frightened." My voice sounded rough from too long underwater using my gills, and I tried again. "I'm a friend. I want to help you."

She seemed frozen in place as I moved toward her. When I emerged almost fully from the water, the small waves near the shore splashed around my ankles, and she slapped a hand over her mouth as her eyes went impossibly wide.

Green eyes like mine.

Glancing down, I realized my erection was on full

display, and she seemed unable to stop staring at it. When her eyes met mine, the female released a nervous laugh, took another few steps back, and held her hands out in front of her.

"I'm not going to hurt you." I wanted to comfort her, but no amount of concentration could get my body to stop responding to her presence and feminine scent—sweat, thicker than usual, I'm certain, but underneath the smell of exertion and fear was the delicate femininity I craved to taste.

I took another step forward, and she took another one back with another bout of nervous laughter.

We couldn't communicate, so how could I explain to her the danger she was in?

I could learn her language if I could touch her mind. I wouldn't need much—a few minutes and a simple touch, and I could get enough of her language to talk to her.

But first, she'd have to let me close enough.

The female started talking, a string of strange syllables. She gestured to the Ghaal colony and moved her hands around, sometimes pointing up or down the beach. I had no idea what she was saying and found my gaze drifting from her face down her body, over her torn clothes, and lingering anywhere I could glimpse her skin.

When I pulled my gaze back to her face, she stopped talking and presented me with a nervous smile that looked unnatural. Her smile fell when my brows drew together.

And she ran.

I didn't stop to think I might scare her. I simply went after her.

CHAPTER 3

MISHA

Have you ever seen a monster movie where the monster is the target of the audience's sympathy? *Aw, a poor, misunderstood monster who only wants to be loved.*

That's all well and good until the monster is seven feet tall and approaching you with a throbbing erect cock, the biggest cock you'd ever laid eyes on. Then survival kicks in, and *obviously*, you don't understand each other. But the way he looks you up and down makes it clear his intentions aren't to hold hands and tell each other stories.

So, you'd run, right?

I ran from the ocean monster, but he came after me. With longer legs and a large muscular frame, even the shock of me running first wasn't enough to give me much of a head start. He gained on me quickly, and when he lunged and grabbed my calves, I screamed as I fell onto the sand.

Rolling onto my back, I tried to get away, only to have him roll on top of me. As he grabbed my wrists and pinned my hands next to my head, he said something again, sounding desperate and angry.

Oh God, what does he want?

I think I had an idea of what he wanted, and I didn't want *that.*

I glanced down to see his cock was still hard and rubbing against my leg. But it wasn't an intentional movement. He seemed to be mostly ignoring his arousal, focusing now on my face and continually talking to me.

When I stopped struggling, he stopped talking.

My chest rose and fell as I panted, trying to catch my breath, and I took a moment to study him. His skin was mostly smooth, although it appeared textured like scales until you touched it. Where his hands grabbed my wrists, his skin felt like a silky rubber. He was the same gray as the ocean but streaked with dotted neon purple, one of the lines going straight down the side of his face and over his eye. My brows pulled together. It reminded me of those little neon fish people kept in fish tanks, the tiny dots on their bodies creating a pattern when you had a big group of them moving around the tank, except purple instead of blue.

But his eyes were a brilliant green, bright and almost out of place with the rest of him. There was soul and intelligence in those eyes. This wasn't a monster. Maybe this was the intelligent species of the planet.

Maybe.

But he looked like he lived in the ocean, not in the little houses I'd seen in the village over the trees.

His purple hair, streaked with the same gray as the ocean, tickled my face as he leaned forward, planted his face in the crook of my shoulder and neck, and inhaled deeply. I couldn't help the nervous giggle that escaped, and I squirmed under his touch. Perhaps he was just another animal, after all. I'd worked with animals before. I simply had to make sure he didn't think I was a threat, food, or a mate, and I'd be fine.

He pulled away, eyes wide with alarm, and my smile dropped. Slowly, his gaze drew to where he held my hands still before he looked back at my face as if he'd just realized he was holding me down.

When he released me, I shuffled out from underneath his hulking form and leaped to my feet, retreating to a safer distance but cautious about running again. Maybe he was more animal than not, and perhaps running triggered something in him, like a dog playing a game.

He spoke again, and I tilted my head. There was nothing familiar about his words, nothing I could even consider close to an Earth language, his tongue and mouth working around the alien sounds.

Pressing my lips together, I took a few tentative steps away from him. A quick glance over my shoulder showed I wasn't far from the rocky outcrop that would lead me to the village. Despite the discovery of this... *man*, I still thought the village was worth checking out.

Fifty yards, give or take, and I'd be at the rocks.

I jutted my thumb over my shoulder. "I'm going that way," I said, knowing he couldn't understand me but needed to do *something*.

The creature shuddered, shaking his head and body and making his hair splash water droplets on the sand between us. His lip lifted into a snarl, and with a jabbing motion, he pointed behind me, then at me, and then snarled again.

I frowned, and he repeated the motion.

When I took another step back, he closed the gap between us with a few well-placed steps that ate the ground beneath him. He grabbed my shoulders, held me still, and stared so intently into my eyes I couldn't look away. He pointed at me, then behind me toward the village, and then growled at me again.

He said something, and I simply answered, my voice small. "Are you trying to warn me of something?"

The alien creature released me, shoved me slightly away from him and, frustrated, stomped around in a small circle. He wanted to tell me something he considered important, and I wished I understood. I didn't want him to get angry, and I also wanted to know whatever it was he was trying to tell me.

When he came closer again, he snaked his fingers through my hair, and tilted my head back. A touch so delicate and intimate, it took me off guard for a moment. He muttered something again, his voice deep and soothing, and I almost fluttered my eyes closed.

"No!" I shoved him away when I felt his erection brushing against me again.

He looked mutinous.

Oh shit, I've pissed him off.

Time stretched out as we stared at each other, neither making a move or speaking. The alien gestured at his head, then at mine, and raised his eyebrows as if asking my permission for something.

My brows furrowed, and I couldn't help another glance at his still semihard cock.

What did he want? To pet my hair or do a Vulcan

mind-meld on me?

Cautiously, as if he were pausing to think before every step, he approached me again. I took one step back for every three of his approaching, and eventually, he ended up toe-to-toe with me. Craning my neck, I looked up to meet his eyes, certain there was intelligence beyond the animal. Again, he gestured at my head, and while I shook my head slightly, I didn't move until he snaked his fingers gently through my hair. When he did this, a quiet rumble worked through his chest, like a growl or a purr, and at the same time, his fingers tightened slightly in my hair.

I jerked away from him, thankful he let go of my hair so it wasn't ripped from my scalp.

Another rush of syllables and clicks left his lips, and he continued to repeat the gesture from my head to his, but this time he also gestured his mouth.

"What do you want?"

My question seemed to excite him, and he enthusiastically waved his arms about.

My head, his head, his mouth, my mouth.

Once again, he approached me, and I tensed as he stopped in front of me. He kept talking to me, and although I couldn't understand the words, the tone was soothing as if *I* were an animal he was trying to tame or calm down. He placed his four fingers against my temple, and a flash of white covered my vision for a split second. It wasn't pain as such but more of a discomfort, an awareness that something had happened to my head. *My mind.*

Immediately, I pulled away and held my hands between us as I shook my head. "What was that? What did you do to me?" There was no longer a sense of an odd feeling, but my vision blurred after the white flash, and panic began to settle in my chest.

"Heh. Tah. Cah." This time, his words were only stilted syllables instead of the steady flow they'd been before, and I slapped a hand over my racing heart. I couldn't understand what he was doing, but the shift from *potentially harmless ocean creature* to *intelligent alien* to *alien who could perhaps erase or control my mind* was too much.

"Stay away from me!" He frowned at my shout and hovered where he was for a beat before he stormed toward me. "*No,*" I cried out and slapped his hands away as he tried to touch my head again. His insistence at the contact ended up pushing me to the sand, and I kicked out and slapped at him. I had no idea if the alien was trying to drug me or *what,* but I wasn't about to let some strange being do any damn thing to my mind. When he eventually stopped trying to touch my head, he instead settled for grabbing both my wrists in one of his hands and held me still as he straddled me.

Another series of jolted sounds was followed by

another string of syllables I didn't understand. It felt like he was losing his cool.

When I continued to try to buck him off me, he snarled, his sharp teeth exposed, and I stilled under his stare. He growled out something that could have been words before he stood and slung me over his shoulder like a caveman. I barely had time to register what had happened before he started running across the beach, back the way I'd come.

"Put me down. Put me *down*." I beat against his back with my fists and kicked my legs against his chest.

The alien stopped abruptly and placed me on my feet. He was gesturing again, throwing his hands up and snarling words at me I couldn't possibly understand. I backed up when he jabbed his fingers to his head, then to mine, and to our mouths again.

"Oh no you don't."

He paced in a small circle on the sand, and I watched him, unsure if I should make another attempt at running. He abruptly stopped and faced me—something was definitely ticking over in his mind, and I was hesitant to think *what* exactly he was planning. With speed surprising for his size, he turned and bolted toward the ocean, lifting his arms above his head to dive gracefully into the water before he disappeared under the surface.

"Okay then..." I muttered.

I waited, but when he didn't return after a few

moments, I took a few cautious steps backward away from the water. Still, nothing happened, so as carefully as I could without appearing to rush, I started walking again toward the village, keeping an eye on the water.

There was no sign of the frustrated alien.

The rocks were further away now, and I cursed the alien under my breath for taking me away from where I'd been headed to get help. I paused when footsteps approached—*running* footsteps—and I spun around just as the ocean alien tackled me to the ground, grabbed me around the waist, and protected me with his body as we rolled. I screamed, only to have his hand slapped over my mouth, the texture of his webbed fingers feeling odd against my skin.

Before I could protest further, he began wrapping seaweed of some sort around my wrists and ankles.

"Oh, you have to be fucking *kidding me*," I said, twisting in an attempt to be released from his hold. But he was efficient at his work, and the knots were a tangled mess I couldn't follow. The seaweed was so dark it almost looked black until the sunlight hit it, and it would get a greenish tinge but felt like rubber. No amount of twisting my arms or legs got it to give way.

As I opened my mouth to yell at the alien to let me go, he shoved a small handful of the rubbery seaweed into my mouth, and I had only a moment to appreciate it was tasteless before he bound the gag with a knot around my head.

He stood, stared down at me and then at the beach behind him, and seemed to be in a state of indecision again.

Okay, you've tied me up. Now what, ocean man?

When he met my gaze, I glared at him, mumbling a string of obscenities through the gag.

I think he got the gist and looked almost apologetic.

Grabbing my arms, he dragged me to the cliff face the beach backed onto, found a small shaded nook, and hid me inside.

What's he doing? Saving me for later? A little midnight snack?

Or afternoon delight?

He jabbed a finger at me, snapped something in his odd language, and watched me glare at him a moment longer before he took off running again.

CHAPTER 4

SAHCOR

Worry tore at my insides as I ran down the beach and, every few moments, debated if I could move faster in the water. Leaving the female alone had been a gamble, but I would reach my goal quicker without her.

And I had to find her unit.

The units scanned the brains of those inside, and if she wouldn't let me close enough to touch her mind directly to learn her language, then I could get it from her unit. She had completely panicked when I had tried to touch her mind—was the head or hair something sacred to her species? A snarl I couldn't help escaped me. How could I even begin to understand when we couldn't communicate?

I'd managed to make the connection for half a second before she pulled away from me, angry at me for even trying. From the brief contact, I'd been able to get only a few syllables but still couldn't say anything she understood.

Hello. Talk. Communicate. I'd found *none* of the complete words in her language. I needed only *one* word to show her what I could do if she let me touch her mind for a few moments more. But the feel of her heartbeat pounding in her chest when I pinned her to the sand stopped me. The female was more than panicked. She was *terrified* of me.

I couldn't let that happen.

When I returned to her after I'd found her pod and could communicate, hopefully, she would accept my apology for tying her up. It was the only thing I could think of. I'd tried to take her with me back to the pod, but she wouldn't allow that either. The moment I stopped running, her heart rate had calmed. She didn't want to be touched or carried, so what else could I do?

Of course, I would explain everything, and then she would stay with me, and I would protect her.

My step skipped a beat when I realized the process my thoughts had taken—I had immediately assumed she would stay with me, something I'd never considered with other rescued species—but beyond that, I *wanted* her to stay with me. I wanted to get to know this strange female.

I wanted to touch her and hear the sounds she made when she was penetrated.

To make her round with my child.

That thought startled me even more as I'd never given much consideration to Synths breeding. But if she was found to be compatible with the Ghaal, then she was with us too.

Maybe I could have a family.

I thought of the other pods that must have fallen and my brothers—there must have been six pods. The Ghaal were a superstitious species and always worked in sixes.

Perhaps we *all* had the chance for families and a future beyond our self-appointed duty.

Putting on a burst of speed, I followed the fading footprints of the female. I knew the language could be downloaded from the units because I had overheard the Ghaal talking about it. My brothers would be horrified to find out—Ilk especially—but I'd been sneaking into the colony every few months for the past four years, listening in where I could and scouting the place. Ilk had a strong stance on no violence, but it seemed to me that, eventually, we might need to fight back rather than passively turning away species.

And now my protective urges had been violently surged into overdrive, and I'm glad I had the knowledge of the colony I did. I knew where the labs were, although there hadn't been activity in a while. I knew there was still conflict between the Ghaal themselves, and killing wasn't unusual.

Even in a time of crisis, they still couldn't find peace.

When the unit came into view, I released a laugh. Soon, I would be on my way back to the female, and we could communicate. Maybe then she wouldn't recoil when I touched her. I'll admit my behavior had been less than ideal, but my frustration at not being understood by her made me angrier than I was prepared for when the stakes were so high.

That, and when she ran, all I could think of was *chase* and *capture*.

And *fuck*.

Luckily, I had enough control of myself not to take that step.

Never without her permission.

The unit sat abandoned on the sand, the tide slowly coming in as it reached closer and obscured what remained of the female's footprints where she'd walked from the unit.

I wasn't there to save or greet her, and she'd wandered lost and alone for too long.

I'd make it up to her.

With a heave, I shifted the unit upright and leaned in. Automatically the unit recognized my Ghaal DNA and began emitting a series of beeps and squeals. Frowning, I reached forward, hoping to find where the language was kept. We weren't very good at technology. I could learn language from her mind easily, but it felt like an incredible violation to tie her up *and* take over her mind.

She'd never trust me again.

This way, I could go back to her prepared.

She'd see how resourceful and intelligent I was.

How much I cared.

It took more time than I'd like, but I managed to connect with the unit's interface the same way I would with a being's mind. With the smallest part of organic matter in making of these units, I could connect to it and learn. I finally managed to get enough of the female's language to be able to communicate with her.

"Hello," I said out loud, rolling the unfamiliar syllables around my mouth. My body would adjust to her language, changing my throat and tongue to speak correctly. "Hello. Hello. What is your name?"

When I thought I had enough to impress her, I took a deep breath and sprinted back toward my female. I tried not to think too much about how she entirely consumed my thoughts. I didn't know her name, the name of her species, or anything about her, but I wanted to impress her, make her happy, and keep her pleasured.

Everything that had happened since I separated from my brothers until the moment I saw her didn't seem to matter anymore. I'd lost myself over the years of being alone and staying alive but not truly living. This was the price I paid, along with my brothers, for doing the right thing and saving innocents.

And I was okay with that.

But with the rush of emotions and desire flooding my body, I still couldn't find myself, and that worried me. I couldn't impress the female if all I could think of was the arousal that fueled my body. Surely, she would want more than that—a companion and a mate.

A family.

Somewhere inside was the Synth I once was, and I'd need to push aside the temptation, ignore the blood that pumped into my cock as I thought of her, and try to remember who I was.

The orange glow of the setting sun was thick on the horizon, casting long shadows from the cliffs that lined the beach. I reached the spot where I'd left the female, clambering across the rocks at the cliff's base, and could barely contain my smile. The expression felt foreign on my face—it had been too long since I smiled.

"Hello? Female?" I called out, turning the corner to where I left her. "I have come to rescue you. Now I can tell you everything. Now we can talk." The words still felt strange, but it wouldn't take long for my tongue and lips to adapt their way around the strange syllables, and for the pause needed when searching my mind for a word to diminish into instant recognition.

I stumbled backward as panic gripped my chest.

The weeds I'd used to tie her lay abandoned on the sand.

She was gone.

MISHA

If I get out of these binds only to run into another alien who tries to keep me captive, I'm going to scream.

With a bit of maneuvering and a lot of chewing, I'd managed to get the gag out of my mouth.

Shuffling around in the grayish sand, I tried to find a way to loosen the rubbery ties from my hands, and I couldn't help the laugh that escaped. It was ridiculous how completely and utterly absurd this situation was. If I didn't laugh, I'd surely lose my mind. I had done my best to keep the other girls entertained while we were trapped on the alien mother ship together, playing silly charades and dancing about like a fool. They may not have been able to hear me, but I was singing songs I made up while doing those dances. It worked for a while, and I thrived on those moments when the fear would subside from their eyes for a short while, and a genuine smile would find its way onto their faces.

But it never lasted long. All it would take was one glance at those horrible little alien men in their space suits, waddling about with their tools and tablets and taking readings but otherwise ignoring us. With only one glance, we'd be reminded of the sick, horrifying reality of our situation.

Now, I was on the beach, tied up by yet *another* alien, and the other girls were nowhere to be found.

Had they seen the little village, too, and headed toward it? I could only hope.

If they hadn't, I would rally a search party, and we would find the other girls. The idea of them being alone out there made my stomach twist.

Especially with giant, horny aliens running around.

My laughter almost turned into a sob before I tugged myself back to my current situation. Lifting my hands to my mouth, I chewed at the seaweed binding my wrists together. It tasted horrible, and I tried not to swallow any of it, and instead nibbled little pieces of the rubbery substance with my front teeth and spat them out. It was slow work, but I could see the ties thinning and the bonds stretched further with every yank of my hands.

Until they finally snapped.

Crying out with relief and elation, I got to work on untying my ankles and clawed at the seaweed until it loosened. I was fit, but I sure as hell wasn't flexible enough to lift my ankles to my mouth and chew those ties off, and I didn't want to slip and crack my head on a rock trying to do so.

Free of the binds, I staggered out of the rocky nook the ocean alien had hidden me in and blinked against the orange glow of the sunlight. It was disappearing over the rocky cliff face behind me. Not wanting to get caught out in the dark, I stopped only long enough to have another drink from the ocean and relieve myself before I took off running toward the rocks, ready to climb them and finally head to the village for help.

Hunger started to tug at my stomach as I made my way through the woods, and I used the trees to support myself as each step became more arduous than the one before.

"Just ten more steps," I said, counting from ten to one. When I reached one and still couldn't see the village, I'd start again. "Just ten more."

My mother used to get me to do it on the rare occasion we ventured to the city and into a shopping mall. The elevators scared the hell out of me, and I'd be fine right up until those giant doors that towered over my head would close, the metal clanging ominously.

"Just count backward from ten," Mum would whisper, holding my hand. *"By the time you get to one, it'll be over."* I'd get to four, and the doors would open to freedom every time.

My parents had moved to the Netherlands two years ago to fulfill one of their retirement dreams. We didn't stay in contact as much as we should have—I was as much to blame as they were—and it might be months before they'd even realize something had happened to me.

I'd done the same thing when the aliens on the ship had me strapped to the table. I squeezed my eyes shut and counted backward from ten. When I got to one and opened my eyes, they were standing around me, having stalled their approach with their instruments of torture and impregnation. I thought I would be let go, and lamely, I held onto the tiniest speck of hope I'd be going home.

Instead, I ended up here.

"Just. Ten. More." I gasped as I slipped and gripped a smooth tree trunk for support. When I got to *one,* I looked up and almost cried with relief when I saw the rooftops of the dwellings that made up the village I'd seen. A burst of energy accompanied me then, and I jogged forward, slowing just enough so I wouldn't stumble down the slight slope that led to the village and stopped at the edge of the hopefully populated area. With a deep breath, I peeked around one of the small houses. It wasn't made of wood, and the metal was unfamiliar and cold to the touch.

Tiptoeing around the edge of the building, I moved into the village, feeling more exposed with every step I took into the open space in the center of the buildings. Even as a cool breeze rolled off the ocean and over the village, I'm certain the shiver that ran down my spine was unrelated.

The aliens came out of the buildings, one or two at a time at first, then almost twenty of them stared at me as I moved into the open. Their eyes were unsettling, the orange rings around the irises looking like some Halloween contact lenses. Their gray skin and hard lips pulled into straight lines didn't move, only their eyes as they tracked my motion.

I stopped and watched them watch me before I folded one arm over my chest and rubbed my upper arm.

They started talking to each other, urgent whispers that set me on edge.

Stepping backward, I intended to leave, only to

back right into one of the aliens. Whipping around, I studied his face. It was so strange, apart from the obvious differences, but I could see our similarities too. It was like someone had taken a picture of a person and smudged it slightly, taking some features and skewing them to be larger or smaller than mine. But still, those eyes and the shape and proportions of their head and bodies were so humanlike I questioned the feeling in the pit of my stomach that I was in danger.

"Hello," he said and grabbed my upper arms as I stumbled away from him in shock, my mind reeling.

"I can understand you," I gasped out.

"Because I'm speaking your language. Don't be afraid… you are safe now."

All the tension melted from my body, and I'm surprised I didn't collapse and fall into a puddle of relief at his feet. The alien looked so strange, but he was an *alien,* right? I was on another planet, and therefore shouldn't be surprised or judge. I bet *I* looked pretty strange to him too. He still held onto my upper arms as I tried to gather my thoughts, and I barely registered how his grip tightened.

"I need help. I was abandoned here…" It was difficult not to ramble. It was imperative they realized the urgency and understood the situation. I tried to keep my voice steady and words clear. "There are others, but I don't know where they are."

"Do not worry, female. We will find the other

women. You are safe."

Alarm pounded inside my head as my inner monologue screamed at me in my mother's voice. *Listen to what people are saying, Misha. Really listen.*

"I never said the others were women..." I whispered, and when I attempted to take a step back, his grip on my arms tightened again until it was painful. "Let me go!"

If I'm captured by one more alien, I swear I'm going to scream.

I opened my mouth to release the scream that was hovering there as terror crawled up my throat when the other aliens approached and enclosed me in a circle of their bodies. A hand slapped over my mouth, I was dragged to the ground before there was a sharp pain, and everything went black.

CHAPTER
6

MISHA

When I woke, broken strips of sunlight cast across my face. Groaning, I rose to a sitting position and rubbed the back of my head. When the realization I was in another cage finally made its way to my consciousness, my instinct was to rush to the bars.

Instead, as soon as I stood, I swayed and leaned out to place a steadying hand on the wall as my stomach churned and bile rose in my throat.

"Don't vomit, don't vomit, do *not* vomit," I repeated to myself. The last thing I needed was the acidic smell of sickness in a cage with me. The feeling slowly subsided, and I took a few deep breaths, trying to calm myself. The air was stale, and I stumbled over to the only window and gripped the bars, ignoring how they burned my hands, and pulled myself to my toes so I could suck in mouthfuls of cool sea air.

Captured. Again.

A series of clicks and clangs, as though chains were being dragged over each other, made me stand at attention, and I pressed myself against the rear of my cell as two of the aliens with orange eyes entered through a door into the hall on the other side of my cell bars. They stopped in front of me, wearing equal looks of self-satisfaction, and their eyes gleamed with menace. I shuddered and crossed my arms over my chest, trying to look disinterested when, instead, I was attempting to offer myself some comfort.

Was this what the ocean monster was trying to warn me about?

Was he trying to keep me safe by tying me up?

Dread crawled under my skin, and I hastily tore myself from my musings and used the orange ring around the irises of my captors' eyes to distract me.

"I bet you're wondering why you're here," one of them said as smoothly as he could with the odd quality of his voice, like an incomplete echo.

"I'm hungry." I stood my ground, although I was backed against the wall, unwilling to engage in conversation with them until I could think straight, and I hadn't eaten in over a day.

"You'll get something to eat once we've asked you a few questions."

"I'm not saying a damn thing until I get some food and fresh water."

I managed to keep my voice steady and could only hope they didn't have some alien senses that could tell how hard my heart was beating and the nervous way I had to keep swallowing. I felt betrayed, and although it was entirely my decision to come into this village, the idea I'd made such a horribly stupid choice hung over me. The only ones I could direct my anger toward were my captors because they had tried to lure me into a false sense of security and forcibly took me when I'd resisted.

It wasn't *entirely* my fault.

But my thoughts kept straying to the ocean alien with his bright green eyes and his strange body language as he tried to warn me about this village. We couldn't communicate, and so he'd resorted to tying me up to keep me safe. I saw that now, but I couldn't help how I reacted. If someone kept you captive, your instinct would be to escape. It's human nature.

The cage bars clanged as one of the aliens rushed at them and gripped them with his gray fingers, making me jump. "You're not in a position to make demands, human. You're lucky I'm not already cutting you op—"

"Now, now." The second alien touched his shoulder and gently pulled him away from the bars. "Let's get her some food, and then she'll talk to us." When he turned to me, I cowered under his gaze. "Won't you?"

I nodded, unable to form words, and as soon as they disappeared through the door at the end of the hall, I sank to the cell floor and cried.

They brought me food and a cold metal container of water. At first, I thought the food was the same thing we were given on the ship, but these were white, rubbery strips that resembled bark. They were nutty but not unpleasant, only difficult to eat. But I took my time eating until I felt satisfied and tried not to look up at the two aliens who watched me the entire time.

When I finished, I pushed myself to my feet and kept as much distance as possible between myself and the aliens.

"Why am I here?"

There was a sound that could almost be laughter from them, and one shook his head. "We ask the questions, you answer. Hesitation or lies will be met with punishment. Do you understand?"

When I didn't answer, he banged his hand on the bars, and I jumped. "I understand."

"Good, humans aren't so stupid after all." They chuckled again, and rage bubbled in my stomach with fear. "You are female, correct?"

"Yes."

"Have you ever birthed a child?"

"Wh—" my words were cut off with a choke at the look they gave me, and I steeled myself. "No."

"Are you capable of bearing children?"

I didn't like how these questions were going and desperately glanced between the two interrogators. Neither of their faces showed any hints of sympathy. I took too long to answer, and one of them began to draw some sort of weapon from his pocket. It looked like a metal stick, nothing more, and I stepped back as he pulled on it and drew it out longer so he could reach me through the bars.

"Are you capable of bearing children?"

"I..." He jabbed forward with the stick, and when it met my skin, I screamed at the searing and abrupt pain. He withdrew the weapon, and I sobbed, the burn on my arm evident even as the memory of the shock tingled through my skin.

"Are you capable of bearing children?"

"As far as I know!" I cried out, then added, quieter as my shoulders slumped, "I've never tried. I don't know."

"But you menstruate?"

"Yes," I answered through gritted teeth as I eyed the weapon.

"Sol will be here soon to ask further questions and relocate you to your permanent residence. You will not resist. We do not wish to kill you."

I said nothing as they left and wondered if death would be better than whatever they had in store for me.

The day passed slowly, and although I'd investigated every corner of my cell, I couldn't find any signs of weakness. There were no locks to pick, gaps to exploit, or cracks in the floor or walls. The only other exit was the window, but it was covered in heavy bars, and the gaps were too small for me to fit through. The bars were made of the same cold metal as the cell bars that separated me from the hallway where the aliens had stood.

When the clanging sounded again, I jumped to my feet and backed into the familiar spot of the rear corner as though that would offer me any protection. A lone alien shuffled in, his hands clasped in front of him and eyes on the floor. I tilted my head, immediately taken off guard at his submissive posture. My horses walked like that when they'd done something they knew was wrong and didn't want me to scold them.

Shaking my head, I straightened my back. I couldn't be taken in by these aliens.

"I am Sol," he said softly as he approached the bars. "If you will talk to me, I have a few questions."

My brows furrowed. He was bordering on asking my permission to speak to me. "Do I have a choice?" I snapped as my gaze automatically sought out to see if he had the same weapon the others had used on me.

His eyes met mine then, and I held his gaze before his eyes flickered toward the closed door behind him. "No, I suppose not."

He came to the bars and held something out between them. Cautiously, I moved toward him, and after staring at it for several seconds, I accepted his offering.

"A pillow?" I asked, and he nodded, indicating the floor. Still weary, I sat cross-legged on the pillow, keeping enough distance that Sol couldn't reach through the bars and grab me in a hurry.

"I have some questions about your friends."

"I don't know where they are," I answered hurriedly, which was the truth. And as much as I wanted to find them, I wasn't going to sell them out to these aliens who obviously meant harm.

His lips pressed together. "I know. That's not my question." He cleared his throat as if this conversation was as difficult for him as it was for me. "When we do find them, we wish to bring them here, but ideally..." He cleared his throat again, a squawking sound emerging this time that made me jump and grip the edge of the pillow. "We would like to do it peacefully."

"Why do you want us?" I whispered. I got the feeling Sol wasn't meant to be talking to me as he was, treating me as a person and more than a prisoner. Asking him questions back seemed like something forbidden, but he didn't threaten to punish me.

"Our species is dying..."

"No." I'd heard all I needed to, stood, and moved to the back of the cell again. "No, *no.* I'm not going to mother some fucking alien baby."

Sol also stood before he faced me. "This will be a lot easier on you... if you cooperate."

"Let me get this straight." When I barged toward the bars, I reveled in the fact he recoiled slightly from me. "You want me to *willingly* allow myself to become impregnated with an alien baby? And then what? I get killed?"

"No, no, not at all. You will birth several children. Tens of children. Perhaps more."

My jaw dropped. "That's not better, Sol!" Hysteria was edging into my voice, and I pointed to the ceiling. "Those other fucking aliens already tried this shit, why would I *let* you do it?"

Sol twisted his hands together. "Please, you are becoming anxious. They will drug you if you do not calm down."

"*Anxious* doesn't even *begin* to describe what I'm feeling!"

"Please!" I jumped back as Sol slammed his palms against the bars. "Listen to me, female, and listen closely. You were not compatible with the Moeks on the ship, but you *are* compatible with us. Now, the Moeks would never perform experiments or surgery to attempt pregnancy, but I can assure you that morality does not exist here. So, you can calm down and let me make this easier, or they will *force* you in more ways than one."

I froze and stared at Sol, and as my lip trembled, he sighed.

After some silence, I asked, "And what makes you different?"

"I wish to... make this process less violent. Now please, I need your help." I scoffed but said nothing, and Sol continued, "*When* we find the other women, we will need to approach them carefully. I do not wish for them to be afraid. I need you to tell me perhaps some human customs, gestures, or greetings that will allow us to gain their trust."

"Essentially..." I croaked the word out before I found my voice. "You want me to help you *trick* my friends into trusting you so you can *use* them for breeding?"

He watched me for a moment. "I can see this is useless. That is unfortunate." He hovered his hand over a silver ball near the bars of my cage. "What is your name?" When I remained tight-lipped, he sighed again. "Listen to me, female, and listen closely. I am about to open this door. You will come to me and follow me to your new quarters. If you try to run, there are Ghaal everywhere."

"Ghaal?"

"Me, I am a Ghaal. It's my species name. We are all over this colony. If you run, they will chase you. We outnumber females fifty to one here. They'll catch you, and they'll keep you in the center of the colony all night, taking turns trying to impregnate you... manually."

I stumbled as though he had slapped me. "And if I follow you quietly and don't run?"

"You will make it to your new quarters untouched and unharmed."

I nodded, although I didn't quite believe him.

Untouched and *unharmed* until they needed to start their experiments.

CHAPTER 7

SAHCOR

It was agony waiting for the sun to set and night to settle over the Ghaal colony so I could go looking for my female. I knew that's where she'd gone. She must have seen it and assumed there would be help there. I cursed myself for not connecting with her mind when I had the chance, but having her struggling and screaming against me while I tried to make the connection made me sick. I never wanted to force her. Tying her up had been hard enough. It was an act that felt wrong to my very core when I was doing it.

I tried to keep her safe, and I failed. I hadn't been

thinking straight, distracted by the surge of hormones and lust that blossomed when I'd seen her.

But I'd been swimming since. I lurked in the ocean just deep enough that the colony couldn't see me and waited for nightfall so I could sneak in.

My brother, Ilk, would be furious if he knew I'd been into the colony and beyond angry if he knew I'd done it more than once, but I knew my way around there and was careful.

I had to be.

The Ghaal had created us, and they could destroy us. A failsafe had been programmed into our DNA, and they had a weapon that worked only on us. If they broke our skin and the formula got into our bloodstream, it would shut us down, one organ at a time, and couldn't be stopped. It was useless against other Ghaal, a weapon created purely to keep us in line.

Because even lab-created beings had a will to live.

Waiting until long after the sun had set and the sounds from the colony had died down, I crept onto the land, kept low, and allowed my skin to become covered in the shore's muddy gray sand. The lab was nearer to the other side of the colony, closer to the mountains, but coming from the ocean was still the safest way.

It took an hour for me to move the short distance

through the colony as I stopped every few steps, remained low, and kept behind buildings and trees.

When I got to the lab, I lowered myself to my stomach, shuffled forward, and peeked through the bars of the basement cell. A blue glow filled the room, although I couldn't see where the glow was coming from. The Ghaal security relied entirely on scouts throughout the colony, their surveillance technology old and useless.

"Female?" I hissed through the bars. There was no answer. The window was not large enough that I could fit through, but I could reach between the bars and try to maneuver myself to see around the quiet space.

Nothing. There was no one there.

I waited for hours, wondering if they hadn't yet brought her here. They would. This was where they conducted their experiments. When the sun's glow came over the ocean, I had to work to keep the growl in my chest quiet. I didn't want to leave the female in the hands of the Ghaal for another day, but I had no choice.

I'd come back tomorrow night, and she would be here.

She had to be.

Returning to the lab the second night, I picked up on her scent before I reached the edges of the building.

She was here.

Crawling across my stomach, I dug up handfuls of loose dirt with my webbed fingers, moved to the prison window as I had last night, and wrapped my hands around the cold bars.

"Female?" I whispered into the cell.

A startled squeak was the only response I got, and I tilted my head to look down. She was leaning against the wall, and when she looked up and saw me, she squealed again and scrambled away from the corner. A dim blue light reflected off the side of her face, casting her partially in shadow as she studied me.

"You!" she hissed out. A number of emotions played across her face—anger, surprise, relief, confusion—before she cautiously stood and moved closer to the window. "Did you just speak?"

"I learned your language. I'm sorry I frightened you."

"How?"

"Your language is stored in the unit you came in. You would've been scanned the moment you were put inside."

She shook her head. "The Ghaal spoke my language too. That doesn't make any sense."

My brow furrowed, and I couldn't understand

what she said. There was no way the Ghaal knew the language. They could build units to read languages, and they could download the information from those units, but not directly from minds like my brothers and I could.

I had the female's unit, not them.

I craned my neck to try to see around the cell. "Is anyone else in there with you? Any other females of your species?"

She shook her head again, looking deflated as though she simply ran out of energy at that moment. "No, thank God. I think I'm the only one they got. They wanted me to help them trick the others into coming here."

"You didn't help them, did you?"

"Of course not!" she cried out and ducked down when I shushed her.

That only raised further questions about how the Ghaal learned her language. Her unit was on the beach, and I hadn't seen any Ghaal near it nor any tracks to indicate they had found it. They can't learn language from a touch like Synths can, and if they had more than one of the females, they had no reason to separate them. That would only create more places to guard.

I shook the thoughts from my head—it wasn't important right now.

"I'm going to get you out of here," I whispered, and my heart thudded louder against the inside of my chest when she took a few tentative steps toward me. Her scent grew stronger beyond the veil of sweat, fear, and grime. It was something distinctly feminine.

"You were trying to warn me," she whispered, getting closer to where I lay with each step. Her face was level with the window, and tentatively, she reached up and placed her hands over mine. My pulse jumped, and my cock hardened, pressing painfully against my stomach at her touch.

Delicate and gentle, her skin was so smooth I wanted to lick and taste her. "You were trying to keep me safe. I'm sorry I ran away."

I could barely form words as my instinct took over, and my body screamed at me to break these bars apart and rescue this female. "You were scared. I understand."

"What's your name?" she asked.

"Sahcor."

She repeated it, tripping over the pronunciation slightly in the middle, but it was close enough. "I'm Misha," she said, and her lips curved into almost a smile, shy and hesitant.

"Hello, Misha."

"Hello, Sahcor."

Unable to resist the urge to touch her, I reached out and cupped her cheek in my palm. She leaned into my touch, closed her eyes, and sighed. With her eyes still closed, Misha whispered, "I don't know how much longer I can stay strong, Sahcor. I'm afraid."

It shattered something inside me, and when I yanked my hand from her face, her eyes flew open, wide and full of fear.

"I'm getting you out of here."

"What? How?"

"I'm going to break these bars." I gripped the metal, flexed, and tested their strength.

"You can't, they're too strong. You'll hurt yourself."

Her concern for me only fueled the animalistic part of me more, and I said, "Stand back."

I should wait, devise a better plan, and find a way to get her out of here that left no traces. The Ghaal would immediately know what had happened—no other being on this planet could break these bars. They wouldn't know it was me specifically, but they'll know it was a Synth. I was exposing our involvement in the species they kidnapped. I'm certain they had long suspected our interference, but I would be cementing their theories by breaking Misha free so soon.

Ilk would want to kill me for this. Lanir would applaud my actions.

I'm not sure how I felt about either of those things.

I was the thinker, the logical one. Despite being a close second to Vitri when it came to almost losing control of myself when we were caged together and tortured, I was generally levelheaded, quiet, and resourceful—all these things Ilk had told me he admired about me when really all I wanted to be was a male of action.

Apparently, all of those traits Ilk admired flew out the window when it came to Misha. I'd failed her once before by tying her up in some lame attempt to keep her safe rather than simply connecting with her mind, and I wouldn't fail again. Despite my actions being impulsive, I could think of no other way.

All I wanted, all I *needed,* was to get Misha out of here and have her with me.

"Stand back," I repeated.

Wide-eyed, Misha did as I asked. She wrapped her arms around her chest and moved away from the window. Gripping the two center bars, I took a deep breath and pulled. Misha took another step back as I grunted, and I took a moment to look at her, taking in the curves of her body visible under her ripped clothes, and used the surge of protectiveness that pumped through my blood to power me forward.

The bars creaked.

Gritting my teeth, I kept pulling, not daring to let go and try to start again, afraid I'd lose any momentum I had. Cracks formed around the joints where the bars were held in place, and with another yank, one of them bent further. Gasping, I let go and studied the gap I'd created.

She just might fit.

Reaching my arms through, I beckoned to Misha. "Come, I'll lift you out."

Misha scampered forward, reaching up without hesitation, and let me wrap my hands around her upper arms. Pressing her bare feet against the inside wall, she pushed upward, and I pulled her shoulders through the gap. Halfway through, Misha grunted as I shuffled backward, and she scrambled against the dirt, trying to maneuver herself free. Crouching next to the bars, I angled her hips to help wiggle her loose, and with a sigh followed by a sob, she became free.

Immediately, she stood and threw her arms around my neck before I could stand too. Her breasts pressed against my face as she hugged me, and in response, I wrapped my arms around her body and deeply inhaled her scent.

Misha's back stiffened, and she glanced down, her eyes going wide as I looked up at her from her cleavage. She pulled away from me, and when she noticed my erect cock, she squeaked again, putting more space between us. "Th-thank you," she stammered out.

I held my hand out. "We have to go."

There was only a moment's hesitation where I saw fear and doubt cross over her face. My heart dropped into my stomach, and I wished I could control my body better. My erection was making her uncomfortable, and perhaps she thought I would force her the way the Ghaal would have. When she took my hand, I wrapped my fingers around hers, and Misha looked at me when we didn't immediately move.

"I won't hurt you, Misha... not ever."

She looked at me as though searching for the truth in my eyes, and finally, she nodded. We ducked down and ran for the cover of the woodlands.

CHAPTER 8

MISHA

Once we were a safe and enough distance from the Ghaal village—according to Sahcor—we switched from a quiet jog into a full-out run. My lungs burned, but I dared not stop, and Sahcor kept a firm grip on my hand as he pulled me along. Every couple of steps he would change his gait, and I got the distinct impression he was slowing down considerably to match my speed. Occasionally, I would put on a burst of speed, motivated by not wanting to increase his discomfort, but it wouldn't last long.

After what felt like hours, I tripped, and when Sahcor caught me, he didn't put me back down.

Instead, he lifted me under my shoulders and legs and cradled me against his chest.

"You don't have to carry me, really," I said, my words coming out shaky as he picked up speed and ducked and weaved between the trees. He skidded to a halt when we reached the rocky outcrop I had climbed over, and the blast of minerally sea air made me gasp and brought tears to my eyes. It was like a view of freedom.

But once we were no longer in the cover of the trees, and the wind battered against my face, stinging my skin, it made me cry out. It was like a miniature tornado, and the waves crashed angrily against the shore as Sahcor raced across the sand in the darkness. The moon was large and cast light across the beach in a breathtakingly beautiful way, not to mention how it played across the purple-dotted patterns on Sahcor's skin, almost making it glow and sparkle. I traced my fingers across the pattern on his chest, distracted for a moment, but yanked my fingers away when he growled deep and low. I glanced up. His expression hadn't changed, but his grip on me tightened, and I remembered the way he had greeted me—his large cock standing at attention and practically pulsing—and decided maybe I shouldn't be delicately tracing patterns on his chest.

I was high on adrenaline, and the combination of the terrifying weather, what I hesitated to admit to myself—a hint of arousal—and the uncertainty of what was to come next only sent me further into the spiral of fear and confusion.

I'd been rescued from the bad guys by my knight in… scaly armor.

Abruptly, Sahcor pivoted and headed toward the ocean.

I screamed as the ice-cold water lapped at me as he ventured deeper, and I grabbed at his neck. Sahcor looked down at me, his eyes wild and hair falling in front of his face, and I gasped. He looked animal-like, the intelligence and empathy I'd previously seen in his face were gone.

"Sahcor, please," I begged, swallowing heavily and glancing down at the waves as they continued to churn around us. "I can swim but not well enough to survive in this."

His expression softened, and my teeth chattered as he lowered me into the water that came up to cover my stomach, whereas it only sloshed around his thighs. Sahcor bent, almost fully submerged himself, and turned, presenting me with his back.

"Hold onto me," he said, raising his voice over the wailing wind and crashing waves.

I glanced around and grabbed his shoulders when a particularly nasty wave almost knocked me off my feet. This was crazy—I wanted to scream and cry. I just wanted everything to slow down for a moment so I could *think.* "I can't breathe underwater, Sahcor. You know that, right?"

"I will go as fast as I can, but we can't keep moving over the beach. We'll leave tracks." Again, I looked nervously back at the shore, seeing where his footprints disappeared into the water. He followed my gaze and grabbed my hand on his shoulder, wrapping it around his neck. "Please, Misha, you must trust me. Hold on tight and take a deep breath. Keep your eyes closed, and I promise we'll surface before you know it."

I don't have a choice, do I? Where was I going to go? Back to the Ghaal? Wander around until they took me again?

Nodding, I leaned forward and wrapped my arms around Sahcor's neck. I gripped my forearms, holding on as tight as I could until the sting of my nails digging into my skin reminded me this wasn't a dream. Sahcor held my eye contact, and I waited for him to say something comforting.

But all he said was, "Deep breath." And I did my best to steady myself to do just that before he dived.

For the second time that night, my lungs were burning. But there was no reprieve this time, and I couldn't simply stop moving and take a few deep breaths. The water rushed around me, every icy touch setting my nerves on fire as I clung to Sahcor's neck. I was putting my life in the hands of this alien. He could easily dive deep into the ocean and let me drown, holding me under until I didn't have the oxygen left to escape.

I tried to push the intrusive thoughts from my mind because panicking right now would do me no good.

But. I. Needed. Air.

I couldn't signal to Sahcor, tap him on the shoulder, or anything because, with the speed he was moving, I was afraid if I let go or lifted my hand, I would go tumbling back into the depths, and he wouldn't find me before it was too late.

Leaning forward, I pressed my lips to Sahcor's neck, unable to think of anything else to do to signal to him. He gave no sign he'd understood me, but I swear I'd felt him change direction. It was impossible to tell which way was up, so I only hoped we were heading toward the surface and not further down.

When we broke free, I gasped loudly, coughing when a wave splashed water into my open mouth. In my panic, I began splashing around, forgetting everything I knew about swimming despite years of swimming in the dam, and instead kicked and flailed madly. Sahcor glided up to me, wrapped his arms around my waist, and lifted me slightly so my head was clear of the water, and I could take a moment to catch my breath.

When I'd calmed, I looked around. I couldn't make out much in the darkness, but it seemed like we were at the edge of a cliff.

"Are we there? Here? Wherever it is we're going?" I asked, and Sahcor's fingers twitched against my lower back.

"Almost," he said, his lip lifting into a slight smile before it dropped, "We have to go under once more." I couldn't control the look of despair on my face, and Sahcor chuckled then. "For seconds, only seconds. We'll duck under the rocks and emerge into the cave where I live."

Any other time, I'm sure that would sound magical, but I didn't have the energy to argue and let Sahcor lower me down and guide me to wrap my arms around his neck again.

"Deep breath," he said, and I complied, closing my eyes as he ducked under the water again.

CHAPTER 9

SAHCOR

Misha loudly gasped as I surfaced into the cave, the silence welcoming after the vicious winds outside and the pounding of the churning ocean in my ears. Gliding through the water with Misha still on my back, I relished the feel of her small body against mine. But she was cold and frightened, and this wasn't the time to linger in the water and learn the shape and lines of her body.

Reaching the cave's shore, I stopped so Misha could climb onto the flat surface. She collapsed onto her back and stared up at the cave ceiling.

"Whoa," she whispered.

The shimmering purple illumination played across her skin, an effect of the crystals embedded in the stone and the moonlight outside. The colors drifted over the water, and the ripples bounced back the light, creating a soothing motion of color across the cave, just enough to break the darkness.

"It's beautiful," she gasped out. I lay down next to her, and while her shivering subsided, her body stiffened for a moment before she relaxed.

I nodded, but I wasn't watching the cave. I was too entranced with *her*.

The lights played gently across her skin, and I wanted to trace the lines they made on her. I wanted to run my fingers over the purple light with an equally light touch and explore her every curve. Her clothes had become partially transparent after our swim, and the peaks of her nipples pushed against the fabric. I shouldn't look, but I couldn't tear my gaze away, instead studying the curve of her breasts.

Misha rolled her head to face me, and my eyes snapped to meet her gaze. If she had noticed me looking at her body, she said nothing about it.

"Thank you for rescuing me." She bit her lip, sat up, and looked around the cave I called home. "Are we... safe here?"

I pushed myself up onto my elbows and continued to watch her. "Yes. They don't know I'm here."

Her wet hair pulled against her skin as she nodded, but her teeth continued to work against her bottom lip. Despite my desire for her, the long swim had given me a chance to clear my head. The cold water had massaged my muscles as I moved and distracted me just enough so I could gather myself and think logically, which I should have been doing from the moment I saw her.

"Were you guarded by the Ghaal?" Her head snapped toward me at the mention of her captors. I pushed myself into a sitting position and shuffled beside her, hoping my presence was a comfort.

"No." She sat, looked at the cave floor, and traced her fingers absentmindedly over the rock. "Not really. They came in now and then to ask me questions or feed me, but I wasn't guarded twenty-four seven."

My brows drew together. I didn't understand what she meant by twenty-four seven, but she'd answered my question regardless, and it troubled me.

"What's wrong?" Her voice broke my trance, and I met her green eyes with mine.

"You were very precious to them. I would've thought they'd have guarded you nonstop."

Immediately, her eyes widened. "You think they *wanted* me to escape? But how? I couldn't have bent those bars."

My lips almost curved at her outburst. My female

was *smart.*

"I think they were open to the idea of you being rescued but not by me."

I expected her to get upset when she realized what I meant, but she slammed her palms against the rocky floor instead. "They wanted the other girls to come and get me. Those *assholes.*" It was impossible not to chuckle at her outburst—smart *and* passionate. Her hair that had slowly dried and formed back into curls, bounced around her shoulders as she glared at me. "Why are you laughing?"

I reached out and rubbed her upper arms. "You're so small and fragile, and you got angry. It was amusing."

She huffed out a breath. "Well, I'm glad you find me so entertaining."

We sat in silence for a few moments, and the tension slowly eased from her body. When she gazed down at where my hands encapsulated her arms, rubbing slowly up and down, she shivered and raised her eyes to mine. I stopped moving but didn't let her go.

Tell me to stop, I thought to myself. *Tell me to stop touching you. You've been through so much. Just tell me to stop, and I will.*

Misha's eyes widened slightly, and when I resumed rubbing her arms, her lips parted in a silent gasp. Her eyes never left mine, and I changed my touch, tracing lines across her skin with my fingertips—four fingers instead of her five. I noticed all the differences as she turned her arm so I could trace lines along the inside of her palm.

But perhaps not so different, not really. She was responding to me, her heart rate increased, and her breath came in gasps. A growl I couldn't help rumbled through my chest as the slightly tangy scent of her arousal hit me. Misha squirmed where she sat but didn't move away.

"You're a beautiful creature, Misha," I pushed the words out, my voice gruff. This time, the puff of breath left her almost as if it were laughter. "You don't believe me?"

She lifted a shoulder. "I'm not wearing makeup, I'm dirty, wet, in torn clothes, and my hair is a mess, so... no." Misha smirked, and my gaze dropped from her face as my exploration moved to her waist.

"What's makeup?"

She chuckled. "I'll explain later."

I hummed. "I don't think I've ever seen another creature as beautiful as you are right now."

"Smooth talker, aren't you?" But her words were a breathy whisper and caught at the end when I boldly cupped her breasts in my palms. I paused, waiting for a protest that didn't come before I gently massaged them. "Sahcor..." her voice edged with warning, but she arched her back into my touch.

Tell me to stop, and I will.

But I hope you don't want me to.

My cock ached, throbbing and hard against my leg as her nipples tightened against my thumbs. Misha trembled again, and I held her eye contact, her pupils darting back and forth as her gaze jumped between my eyes. I was torn between asking her permission to touch her and breaking the spell that had fallen over us. She was exhausted. I should let her rest, but she must have felt some attraction toward me, otherwise she'd be protesting, right?

When another shudder ran down her spine, the idea she might be frightened of me hit me, cemented in my mind, and refused to be pushed to the side.

Maybe she's not saying no because she's scared of you.

I wrenched backward, twisted myself away from her, and dropped my hands from her body. The spell was broken. Misha crossed her arms over her chest, and a pink flush rose to cover her cheeks as she looked at the ground.

"I'm sorry, Misha," I said as I stood and moved away from her. "I didn't mean to scare you."

"I wasn't scared..." she whispered and looked up at me, blinking through the confusion on her face. When I held out a hand to her, she took it, and I pulled her to her feet.

"You need to rest."

Misha simply nodded and followed me to the rear of the cave.

MISHA

My attraction to this alien made no sense, and I huffed out a frustrated breath as I rolled over until my back was facing him, staying close for his warmth. Sahcor had guided me to lie in a bed of what looked like dried seaweed, a mixture of blacks, grays, and browns. I'd expected it to be scratchy and uncomfortable, but it was surprisingly soft. As I'd snuggled deeper, it turned out to be good insulation, keeping me warm even as my clothes finished drying.

Sahcor lay down next to me, his large form distracting. Despite our differences, there was no denying the pure animal magnetism about him—his sculpted arms, chest, wide shoulders, large muscular thighs, and the way his hands encompassed my waist and then my breasts as he explored me.

Huffing out again, I grit my teeth as I shuffled back against Sahcor.

"Misha?"

"I'm a bit cold," I replied and listened to the shifting of the seaweed under us as he rolled over, pressed his chest against my back, and draped an arm around my body, pulling me closer to him. He hesitated a moment before he touched his forearm to my stomach, and I held my breath, waiting for the sparks to fly across my skin at the moment of contact as they had before.

Letting my mind wander, I tried to sort out my feelings.

The only thing that made sense and explained my physical response to Sahcor must have been a result of the trauma I'd faced over the past few weeks. Being abducted, held captive, and escaping over and over again was bound to take some sort of toll on me. I hadn't dealt with it yet because every moment on this planet was about survival. I hadn't had a *chance* to think about it. Wasn't there something about people being attracted and aroused during times of extreme stress?

I wasn't a pushover, didn't cry often, and rarely backed down from a challenge.

But that thought right there—that one wrenched a sob from me.

Every moment on this planet is about survival.

On this planet.

I wasn't just abducted from my home but taken from *my* home *planet,* and I may never get back. Even when people started looking for me, maybe my students from my riding school and their parents when they rocked up to my farm for their lesson on Saturdays, or maybe my parents when they eventually reached out and I didn't respond. Even when that happened, they'd never find me. There'd be no ransom call or means of communication, and escape from one captor had only left me with the new problem of trying to find a way to survive.

I trusted Sahcor because I had to. He'd been the only one who didn't seem to have malicious motives.

But I wasn't stupid—he wanted me for sex. He was attracted to me, and I hated that I was attracted to him too, and I didn't know why. I wasn't the sort to fall for a guy just because he was nice to me, but this wasn't an ordinary situation.

So how could I be sure any feelings I had were even real?

"Misha..." Sahcor's voice was a soothing rumble against my back, and I hadn't even realized I'd been crying until he brought me back to the present moment.

"Sorry," I whispered, reaching up to wipe the tears from my face. "Dammit, I'm sorry."

"Don't apologize, Misha. You're allowed to be sad."

I let loose a watery chuckle. *Sad* didn't seem a strong enough word to explain the hole that was opening up within me. The realization that everything I had taken as a given and for granted was gone, including my horses—and *oh, my Charlie*—my life on my farm doing what I loved—my freedom, my home, my clients, my family, my community.

It was all gone.

Sahcor's arm tightened around my stomach, pulling me impossibly closer to him. Instead of fighting it, I snuggled against his warmth, wiggled against him until his body curved around mine, and let myself cry until I fell asleep.

CHAPTER 10

MISHA

Warm and comfortable, I slowly woke and pulled a face when I stretched my arms above my head. I needed a shower or a bath. Swimming in the ocean was no substitute, and although this ocean wasn't salty like home, it was full of strange minerals which I could only assume came from the rocks and the land the same way salt did. My hair was dry and frizzy, and I could feel a layer of residue on my skin. Darting out my tongue, I licked my lips—they also tasted like the ocean water.

Rubbing my eyes, I stared at the ceiling of Sahcor's cave. It looked different in the natural light. The magic of the moonlight playing through the purple was gone, but the sunlight played its own tricks, and the cave was still beautiful.

My heart skipped a beat when I realized I was looking forward to exploring it. It felt odd to be looking forward to anything, given my circumstances.

Sitting up, Sahcor was nowhere to be seen, and my sense of elation evaporated as quickly as it had formed. Suddenly, the gentle sloshing of the water against the sides of the underwater cave entrance wasn't soothing but a reminder I was alone in the middle of the ocean.

"Sahcor?" There was no answer. I stood and brushed my hands vigorously across my face and arms before I shook out my hair, trying to feel a bit fresher. "Sahcor?" I was only willing to shout so loud, not feeling safe here without him.

Convincing myself he must have gone out for food, I began looking around the cave. I really needed to pee, but it seemed wrong to do it on the rocks near where we had slept or in the lake of water covering most of the cave. There were multiple nooks, some only big enough for me to step into, and others opened up to winding pathways I dared not explore alone.

I'm guessing I waited for about half an hour, and being surrounded by the sounds of water did nothing for my need to relieve myself. Eventually, I drank some ocean water, and although it seemed counterproductive to my predicament, I was thirsty.

When Sahcor returned, I was sitting on the edge of the lake, dangling my feet in the water. The only warning I got that he was back was a glimpse of the neon-purple pattern of his skin moving through the water before he burst through the surface, and I let loose a scream I couldn't help.

He was smiling, and although my brows furrowed, it was nearly impossible not to smile back at him. The look was contagious, like he'd gone through a change overnight and had opened up when the sun rose.

"You're awake," he declared and slapped some fish on the cave floor next to me. "I wanted to let you sleep."

"What time is it?" He stared at me blankly, and I suppressed a laugh. "Never mind."

"Around time to eat again, judging by this," he said and rubbed his stomach. "You slept through the morning meal."

"Sahcor—"

His expression turned dark for a moment as he emerged from the water, and I gasped as his cock came level with my face. Even flaccid, it was impressive, and when he noticed me staring, his cock gave an interested twitch in response to my attention. I cleared my throat, but Sahcor started talking and crouched beside me. "There is a lot I have to tell you, Misha, much of it you have already learned and not the way I wished you to."

"Sahcor, pleas—"

"We'll eat, and then we'll talk—"

"Sahcor, I *really* need to pee!" He stared at me until I squirmed under his gaze. My lip started twitching, and I couldn't stop it, eventually letting loose the laugh I couldn't hold in any longer. I shoved gently at his shoulder, giggling. "Stop staring, you creep, and tell me where I can go to the toilet."

Sahcor stood and moved to the back of the cave, and I hurried to follow, cupping my hand between my legs. This was ridiculous, and I laughed as I waddled after Sahcor. I swear I hadn't had to pee this bad since a hike in summer camp. I hadn't wanted to go in the bushes in front of the mean girls and have them make fun of me. I wish I had, though, the alternative being that I wet myself in front of everyone, and it's not something an eleven-year-old gets over quickly.

Looks like history was about to repeat itself.

I should have just gone in the damn water.

Sahcor pointed at the rear of a cave to one of the nooks I'd found earlier but thought nothing of. There was enough space to stand in and a hole that went downward into the darkness.

"Where does it go?" I asked.

Sahcor smirked. "Deeper, then eventually breaks down. Is this important right now?"

"No, no, I guess not." I waddled forward, shooing him away with the hand that wasn't clutched between my legs, and moved to pull my pants down.

I was laughing and trying to do my business, hoping to get somewhere near the cave toilet before my entire bladder emptied over my clothes.

As I emerged from the nook, I shook my hands out. "Well, that was almost a disaster."

Sahcor looked up from where he was cleaning the fish. "What happened?"

"I almost didn't make it."

We stared at each other for a moment, and he seemed unsure what to make of the situation before he slowly said, "You urinated on yourself?"

I held up a finger. "Correction, I *almost* peed on myself."

"Why didn't you find somewhere to go when I was out?"

"Damn, Sahcor, this is your home. I couldn't just pick some random place to pee. What if I peed on some sacred rock or something?"

His green eyes shone as he looked at me from the constant motion of the light reflecting off the water as it played over his handsome face. For some reason, it irritated me that I found him attractive. I almost wished he looked like the *Creature from the*

Black Lagoon, then I wouldn't be so tempted.

Although, I had always had a soft spot for that creature.

Oh Lord, I'm glad no one could hear me think those two things in succession.

When he burst out laughing, I was taken aback, torn between wanting to be annoyed at his mirth and being unable to stop laughing myself.

"Sacred rock?" He chuckled, and I shrugged, still grinning. "Come, Misha. I'll prepare you some food, then I'll take you to bathe."

"You know what?" I stomped over to him, crossing my arms over my chest as I sat next to him. "I *wished* I did smell like pee. It would be your punishment for making fun of me."

Sahcor's eyes seemed to search my face for a moment as if to check if I was angry, his eyes taking in every line of my expression. He smirked, and I relaxed, having to remind myself again this was an alien being on an alien planet, and perhaps I shouldn't be so blasé about things.

For all I knew, coating myself in urine would have been nothing short of a mating dance.

Sahcor seemed genuinely unbothered, but I apologized anyway. "Sorry, Sahcor, I really didn't mean to make a mess in your home."

"I know you didn't... no need to apologize. I should have shown you last night, but..."

But we were busy as I let you feel me up like a

randy teenager on prom night.

"It's okay," I said.

It's okay.

It's okay that you touched me.

It's okay that I liked it.

It's okay that I wanted more.

Sahcor handed me a slice of fish, and I was about to turn it down because it was raw, but caught myself at the last moment before I hurt his feelings. He was feeding and taking care of me.

"What the hell," I said, taking it and sniffing it. "I like sushi."

Placing the thin slice of flesh on my tongue, I hummed. It had the same mineral quality the water did, and beyond that, it was almost spicy. It was delicious. Humming my appreciation, I returned Sahcor's smile as he sliced the rest of the fish up and sat back to eat with me, letting me help myself. I didn't realize how hungry I was and probably ate two whole fish, offering Sahcor an apologetic look. But he simply smiled and gestured at what remained.

"I'm full, but thank you. That was delicious."

He nodded, scooped up the rest—bones and all—and shoved it into his mouth and chewed gratefully.

"So..." I traced my finger across the cave floor. "You said you had a lot to tell me."

Sahcor's green eyes studied me again, and I

shivered under his gaze, unable to stop my body from responding. "There isn't much pleasant in this story, Misha."

"So, let's get it out of the way. Then you can show me where I can wash up."

SAHCOR

I told her everything.

Misha sat in silence and let me talk, even reaching out and patting my knee when I explained to her how we were created for breeding, capable of advanced learning and adaptation, including changing our gender. I told her how we escaped when we realized the full extent of violence and degradation the Ghaal were willing to go to force us to cooperate. I then shared with her about the species kidnapped over the years and the Ghaal's next plan to help save their own species and how my brothers and I separated from each other to keep the displaced species safe and away from the Ghaal.

"And there's no way to send them home?" Misha asked, and I saw the real question behind her eyes.

Is there a way for me *to get home?*

I shook my head, and her shoulders dropped. "No. We've been cut off from intergalactic trade because of the Ghaal's actions. The only way they got species in the first place was by engaging the services of pirates, desperate for supplies and fuel. You're not even supposed to be here, and we have no way of communicating with anyone who'd be able or willing to take you home."

"I wasn't only asking about me," she whispered, traced her fingertips across the cave floor, and looked down in what I'd realized was a nervous action.

I waited until she looked at me before I said quietly, "It's only natural you would ask."

When her eyes met mine, I couldn't read her expression and wished I could say everything I wanted to. *I like having you around. You remind me of who I once was. You give my life purpose. I see a family with you.* But none of those things were important right now. Misha needed to know the facts, and there was no point in burdening her further with my wishes.

Especially if her wishes were not to stay with me.

I assumed she would want to find the other females she was taken with and perhaps start a colony of their own. But the selfish part of me didn't ask because I wanted her to tell me these things herself, and I wanted to be wrong. Until she did, I could pretend that perhaps having her stay with me was a real possibility.

Squeezing my eyes shut, I didn't know how to feel.

I was meant to be logical, and here I was fooling myself into thinking Misha might feel something for me beyond the one who liberated her from her captors.

"Your brothers and you giving up your lives to protect others is very noble and kind of you."

"We did the right thing."

Misha tilted her head and smiled. "Still, it's an amazing thing to do. Not everyone is willing to give up everything, including their family and dreams to save others, complete strangers, no less."

I nodded, unsure what to say. It had been a long time since I thought of my brothers and how it felt in the brief time we lived together after we escaped. I missed them, and most times it was easier to take every day at a time than to reminisce on how much I had missed. I bet Vitri would never be short of something to say. He would have had a quip or a joke and have Misha laughing with him. The idea sent a pang of jealousy through me, an ugly emotion I shouldn't be feeling at all. I had no claims over this female.

And yet, I remembered the weight of her breasts in my palms, the hardening of her nipples, and the quickening of her breath. She had *allowed* me to touch her.

She was mine.

Now, I simply had to win her over and hope she stayed.

CHAPTER II

SAHCOR

Misha was pacing in circles by the time I finished my story—the idea she was a pawn in the Ghaal's greater plan was likely playing on her mind. After a few minutes of silence, she whipped around to face me and dropped her hands to her sides in one motion.

"This is a lot to take in," she said.

"I know. I'm sorry."

"Not your fault, Sahcor. You don't need to apologize." Misha waved a hand at me and paced for a few steps before she turned to face me again where I sat on the cave floor. "Okay. I think if I keep thinking about it too much, it's going to drive me crazy. There's nothing I can really do about it now. I was abducted to be used for breeding and after the... Mooks, was it?"

"Moeks," I corrected, watching her. I was happy for the opportunity to see how she moved and how her hair bounced around her shoulders as she turned.

"And after the Moeks found we weren't compatible *without* surgery, a step they aren't willing to take, they palmed us over to the Ghaals, the ones who originally ordered the kidnapping of random species across the galaxy, hoping to find one they *could* use."

"Yes."

"But unlike the Moeks, the Ghaal *are* willing to perform not only surgery but experiments to get us pregnant to continue their species." Misha's expression twisted into one of disgust. "But they didn't try to experiment on me. They asked me questions about my ability to get pregnant and where the other girls were." When she turned to me, my mind was already reeling. "It was like they already *knew* I'd be a match for them, you know?"

"And they knew your language."

Misha nodded. "Yes, and how did they learn that if *you* had my escape pod?"

Usually, my role was to tell abducted species only enough to keep them away from the Ghaal, but

I was enjoying this type of conversation with Misha—it was something I hadn't had in a long time. Although the topic was far from pleasant, the way our words bounced back and forth as we worked together to fit the puzzle pieces into a pattern pleased me.

"And you saw no other humans there?"

"None. None of the girls I knew from the ship. No one else at all."

My brows drew together. The Ghaal colony was in disarray, deteriorating over the generations as their numbers dwindled, and those with the knowledge to maintain their technology died too. Most of the specialists had left with the purge a generation ago in an attempt to find the answer on another planet, in another galaxy. So, they had limited technology now.

Whatever they did have was in the main lab where Misha was kept.

What reason would they have for splitting it up over several buildings? None I could think of.

Unless...

"What if..." Misha fell to her knees in front of me, slapping her palms on the cave floor. "We weren't the first humans?" Her words echoed my thoughts from a moment before.

"It would explain how they knew your language and were sure you were compatible."

"Ugh." Misha flopped onto her side, looking up at

me. "One second, I'm telling myself not to think about it, and the next, I'm *overthinking* it." She sat upright, and I loved how she was constantly moving, full of energy that was contagious. "There's nothing I can do, right?"

You could find your friends and start a life here. The words were on the tip of my tongue, but I didn't say them. Misha had told me I was kind and noble, and here I was holding back on saying something that would be important to her. "You just need to stay safe."

"Right," she said before she rubbed her hands down her face. When her eyes appeared over her fingers as she dragged them down, she found my gaze, and I could tell she was smiling before I even saw the curve of her lips. "How about that bathing you spoke of?"

I stood, and a satisfied growl rumbled through my chest when Misha stood, too, and stood so close to me we were almost chest to chest. "It's a bit of a walk."

"Don't we need to swim to shore?"

"These caves connect to the mainland via a narrow peninsula, but it's a maze."

Misha pouted. "If the caves connect to the mainland, why did we swim here last night?"

"To cover our tracks." *Isn't it obvious?*

"Right, right." She rubbed her forehead. "Sorry, not thinking straight. Too much information all at once. A bath will clear my head." Misha looked down at her body and grabbed the fabric of her clothes between her fingertips, pulling it away from her torso. "Don't suppose there's a way to get me fresh clothes, is there?" Her gaze shot to mine before lowering and tracing over my body. I didn't wear clothes and hoped it wasn't offensive to Misha. I understood my nakedness had frightened her in the beginning, but that was probably more my arousal than anything. Even now, under her wandering gaze, my cock twitched, ready to harden for her.

"I'll make you some." She stared at me for a moment, and I got the feeling she was assessing me, taking in every expression, change on my face, inclination, and tone in my voice, and making a judgment on that. My lip twitched—she reminded me of me. "Shall I carry you?" I bent down, offering my back to her. I wanted to feel the curves of her body pressed up against me, another selfish urge I had.

"How far is it?"

"Not too far, but the rocks might be hazardous for you."

"How about I at least try, and if it gets too much, you can carry me?"

Nodding, I moved off toward the rear of the cave, following the curve of the rock, and gestured for Misha to follow me.

MISHA

Usually, I think things through.

But apparently, after all the shit from the past few weeks, I was willing to blindly follow an alien into an entrance hidden between two rock faces. It was instantly dark when we turned the corner, sunlight having nowhere to peek through the rocks, and I reached forward and grabbed Sahcor's arm. He stilled, and I followed the lines of his muscles with my fingers, trying desperately to ignore how good they felt until I found his hand. Wrapping my fingers around his, I squeezed gently.

"It's dark," I whispered, unsure why I was even whispering.

"You can't see in the dark?"

"No. You can?"

There was silence, and I released a nervous laugh. "If you're nodding, I can't see you, Sahcor. I can't see shit."

"There's no shit to see. We release waste where I showed you earlier."

This time, I burst out laughing, the sound echoing off the walls and making me clamp my mouth shut. "No, I mean, I can't see anything."

Sahcor squeezed my hand. "I'll move slowly, just keep your right shoulder to the wall and follow the curve."

Nodding, I followed as he started walking again.

The *bump, bump, bump* of the rough stone on my shoulder was somewhat comforting, reminding me I wasn't about to fall into some invisible abyss. The stone became smooth in places, and I could only assume this was where that purple crystal intertwined with the rock. I bet it was beautiful if only I could see it.

One foot in front of the other, one step at a time.

I followed Sahcor as he turned a corner I couldn't see and another. Horribly lost at this point, I squeezed his hand tighter, aware that if I lost him, I'd probably never find my way out. Sahcor was now my safety blanket. He'd taken on the role of my protector and caregiver, and I'd let him without an argument or fight. I'd looked into his eyes and saw a gentle being I could trust, like my horses.

Some people found horses frightening, and I suppose they were quite large—big forms of muscle that could cause damage if they wanted to or if they were frightened and acted unpredictably. But you be gentle with them and put your trust in them, and they'll do the same for you.

Sahcor wasn't an animal like that, but there were elements to him that were certainly more animalistic than I was used to when it came to men I could have an intelligent conversation with. The nudity was one thing, but the way his arousal was on display, and he seemed unbothered by it, was animal.

And kinda hot.

Brushing the thought away, I focused on the feeling of his hand and rubbed my thumb around the inside of his palm before I worked my fingers gently over the webbing between his large fingers. The webbing didn't go all the way up, just enough to help propel him when he *was* swimming. The ability to breathe in and out of water was fascinating. He had told me that his species—the Synths—were created to adapt. So, the gills, webbing, and texture of his skin were all things that changed over time when he chose to live in and around the ocean.

Amazing. He was an incredible species and an incredible male.

I wondered if his brothers had found the other girls as Sahcor said they would have and if they were safe. There was a pang in my chest as I thought of them. Whenever they came up in conversation, I could see Sahcor studying my face, waiting for the moment when I would ask him to help me find the others or tell him I was going on my own.

But it wouldn't happen. I would never ask.

Because the Ghaal knew I was here and seemed to think they could use me to find the others, I'd never give them the chance. If I stayed away from the other girls, and they never knew where I was, then they wouldn't be in danger from the colony.

So, it now looked like it was Sahcor and me.
And a big part of me found that just fine.

CHAPTER 12

MISHA

Raising my forearm to my forehead, I squinted as the sunlight assaulted my eyes. After the darkness and twisting turns of the cave, the sun seemed brighter than it had the day before. When my eyes adjusted, I glanced around. The ocean spread out to either side of me, and a strip of the mainland reached out into the water, covered in knee-high wispy plants the color of wheat. Dotted around were trees, tall and thin with white bark and ending in flared-out foliage like paint brushes that had been used too vigorously. The ocean air was refreshing, and the shore looked so far away. But it was peaceful, so I took a few deep breaths and closed my eyes.

When I opened my eyes, Sahcor was looking at me, and abruptly, I became aware of the feeling of my fingers wrapped around his palm. We were still holding hands, and I felt self-conscious when I had no business feeling like that, so I dropped the contact. It felt like high school with Sahcor—discovering feelings you'd never had before and resisting the urge to turn away and blush whenever a boy looked at you too long.

Perhaps because it *was* all new, this wasn't home, and Sahcor wasn't even human.

"Come," Sahcor said as he stepped through the grass. "There's a freshwater stream. We'll fill the water bags."

I hadn't even noticed he'd grabbed them before we left and felt guilty for not offering to help as I watched them move across his back where he'd slung them over his shoulder, made of some kind of leather. If I were going to live here, I needed to pull my own weight. That meant learning the ropes—what was and wasn't okay to eat, hunting and fishing, gathering water and supplies—everything.

The stream wasn't far, and I sighed when the trickling water reached my ears. As if this place couldn't be any more peaceful, there was that sound, another thing that reminded me of home—the creeks in the woods around the farm I used as a riding school, the faint rustle of creatures in the tops of the trees, and the scarce undergrowth. There was no background noise beyond the crashing of the waves from the ocean—no traffic, no music, nothing.

And it was beyond peaceful—it was invigorating.

It was almost enough to forget the Ghaal were there on the shore, off in the distance of the horizon.

Almost enough.

Before we reached the stream's edge, Sahcor stopped and dug up some grass, pulling it by the roots. Brushing the soil off, he held them in front of me, and I took one of the clear berries in my hand. "For eating?" I asked.

"You can eat them," he said, smiling, "But the oil inside is good for washing too. It's sterile."

"Fascinating," I murmured.

If I kept saying that, I might have to ask Sahcor to start calling me *Mr. Spock.*

> *Star date, unknown.*
> *I find myself wandering the shore with an alien I'm struggling not to picture having sex with. It doesn't help his considerable member is on constant display, redirecting my thoughts from survival to multiple orgasms.*
> *Science Officer Misha signing off.*
> *Blee-oop.*

Careful, Misha, your nerd is showing.

Hesitating on the stream's edge, I peered into the crystal-clear water. A layer of what appeared to be a mossy undergrowth under the water, thick and a deep blue, only added to the water's crystalline effect. I hummed, shuffling forward and dipping my toes into the water. Cool, but not too cold.

This was going to feel amazing.

"Any creatures in here I should know about?" I asked.

Sahcor was unloading his water bags from his shoulders and dropping them to the ground. "No," he said as he stepped into the water, already naked because, apparently, he was *always* naked. "A few small fish, but nothing to worry about."

I reached down to grab the hem of my top, pausing when I saw Sahcor's eyes on me, his large cock twitching to life. Getting naked with Sahcor seemed like it could be a bad idea, but for better or worse, I felt safe with him. But if I were being *truly and completely honest* with myself, the kind of honest you don't even want to admit to yourself, then I'd admit I wouldn't mind if he touched me again.

And maybe I wanted to touch him back.

Squeezing my eyes shut for a moment, when I opened them, I met Sahcor's intense gaze, and without another word, I pulled my top over my head and dropped it to the ground. It didn't take much shimmying to get out of my pants, shredded and thin as they were cut from the Moek's exploration on the ship. Fully naked, I stood for a moment, the breeze's chill, coupled with Sahcor's wandering gaze, sent a wave of goose bumps across my skin. My nipples hardened, and my hands gripped into fists by my side as I steeled myself to get into the water and closer to what was, at this moment, the ultimate temptation and taboo. I didn't try to cover myself, and after a sweep of my body, Sahcor's eyes came back to rest on mine.

His pupils were blown out, the black almost swallowing the green, and a quick glance down told me how aroused he was, the clear water doing nothing to hide his erection.

Taking a deep breath, I stepped into the water and crouched so I could scoot in without slipping down the bank. The moss was soft, and I curled my toes against it, smiling at the sensation. Fully in the stream, the water came up to my belly, and I faced Sahcor's impressive chest. He was still watching me, and I waited for him to say something, but while it seemed there was a world of thoughts in his mind, he was an alien of few words. Instead of talking, he grabbed one of the root berries near the shore and held it out for me. When I put out my hand, he squeezed the berry, and it burst, releasing a clear, oily liquid into my palm that smelled faintly like sweet fruit. Grateful, I immediately started washing my hands and arms, moving up over my shoulders and groaning as the grime lifted from my skin. The gentle flow of the water took the dirt away, and I kneeled so the water was around my neck.

"Can I have some more berries, please? I'm going to wash my hair."

Again, Sahcor didn't say anything but reached to grab more berries. He wasn't washing himself but simply watched me with an intense gaze that tore me between wanting to hide under the water and filling me with a sense of elation at my effect on him. I wasn't a stranger to the attention of men, but I doubt any of them took me seriously. I think I was the fantasy—the country girl or the girl next door. The sort of girl men would leave the city for, go to a small pub where only farmers and locals hung out, and hope they could blow the mind of some naïve woman who'd never been *lucky* enough to have a taste of *big city cock.*

It was all bullshit, of course, but maybe I was using them as much as they were using me, playing the part they wanted me to play. But I'm certain they wouldn't look twice at me if I weren't the fantasy they were looking for. I was too tall and lanky, my legs were too skinny, and my face was too covered in freckles.

But Sahcor stared at me like a man starving. He'd told me I was beautiful earlier, and while I appreciated it, a part of me believed he was basically flirting, seeking out the same thing most men in my experience had.

I didn't think that anymore.

His jaw was tense, and his gaze flickered from my face down my body and back up like he wanted to stare but didn't want to offend me. He was controlled enough to hold the berries in his hand without bursting them, but the working of the muscles in his neck was telling a different story. Sahcor had explained to me everything about himself—he was *designed* for breeding, his body literally made to procreate, full of urges and hormones he had little control over. He'd been alone for so long that he'd been able to forget that part of himself.

But *I* was changing that for him.

Me.

It seemed unreal.

After the silence encompassed us, falling over us like a blanket and making every other sound of the wild seem exaggerated, he still hadn't passed me the berries, and I stood and held my hand out.

"May I have the berries, please?" He still didn't move, his eyes glued to my chest until I cleared my throat. "I need to wash my hair," I repeated. But this time, my voice was slight under the heat of his gaze, and his body betrayed *exactly* what was on his mind. It was hard to think.

"I'll wash your hair," he finally said, his voice strained.

"Um…" I considered protesting, but I reminded myself this was the beginning of my new life. Him and me because the other girls were safer without me around with the Ghaal on the hunt for me, intent on using me to find them. "Okay," I whispered. Turning, I kneeled again, leaning backward to dunk my hair before straightening again. The water sloshed over my back as Sahcor kneeled behind me, and my senses were on high alert to the point where the break of the berries' skin almost made me jump. He dribbled the oil over my hair and used his fingers to comb it through. Humming, I relaxed into his touch, tilted my head back, and let the sun warm my skin as I closed my eyes. Sahcor massaged my head and worked the oil into my scalp before concentrating on the ends.

"How flexible is that stuff you made your bedding out of?" I mused.

"Fairly, it's what I'll be making your clothes from."

I hummed as he rubbed the tension from my neck and shoulders. "Good, I can use it as a tie and braid my hair."

Sahcor said nothing, and his hands moved down to my shoulders. More oil fell onto my skin, and he worked that in, rubbed away the weeks of dirt and sweat, and washed away the fear and horror of my previous situation. Now, it was just him and me, and a bubble of excitement flared in my stomach. I had lost a lot, but had much to look forward to here. There was much to learn and explore, and if this were to be my life, maybe it was time to seriously consider Sahcor as more than a protector and a friend.

Could a relationship with an alien man really be a possibility?

I guess we had all the time to figure it out.

CHAPTER 13

SAHCOR

After I had washed Misha's hair and back, she dunked herself under the water again, working her fingers through the strands of her dark hair before standing. She reached up to squeeze the excess water from her hair, and her breasts shifted as she lifted her arms above her head, and once again, I was mesmerized.

I'd never been tempted by another abducted species as I was by her. Countless species had been taken, but I'd done my duty and saved as many as I could, haunted by the ones I couldn't protect. If Misha's and my theories were correct, and she and her friends weren't the first lot of humans taken and were compatible with the Ghaal, then she was also compatible with me.

But no matter how much I tried to reason through my thoughts and feelings and tell myself all of these reactions were only chemical, it didn't help. It didn't stop the urges. If anything, it only made them worse, and I began picturing Misha rounded with my child as I cradled her in my arms. Reason didn't stop the warmth that bloomed in my chest, setting off a contented growl I couldn't control whenever we spoke and laughed.

My duty was to protect her, but it was already more than that. Even after such a short time together, I already knew I'd do anything to protect her. I'd kill or lay down my own life.

For my mate.

No amount of reasoning could push the thoughts of her being my mate from my mind. Once the thought was there, it was stubbornly planted and bent around any way I tried to logic my way out of it.

And watching Misha move in the water as she bathed, I gave up trying to reason with myself.

"Your turn."

Her words broke me from my musings. "Sorry?"

She slapped her hand gently against the surface of the water. "Sit. I'm going to wash your hair now."

I swallowed, ready to tell her *no*, that I didn't

think I could stand to have her hands on me. Washing her hair was almost too much, but I couldn't stop. Even wanting to say no to her now, I found myself sinking to my knees, holding her eye contact as I sat on the bed of the stream, studying her green eyes as my face became level with her breasts.

She laughed. "Turn around."

I did and wet my hair as she had. I occasionally bathed here but mostly relied on swimming in the ocean to keep clean. The minerals in the water kept my skin smooth, and I absorbed what I needed from them through my pores. It hadn't worked for Misha, and they'd sat on the surface of her skin, creating a dusty covering. So, I guessed we'd be coming here to bathe more often.

A satisfied growl rumbled through my chest at the thought, and I smiled.

"Why do you do that growl thing?" Misha asked as she squeezed the gladvin roots over my hair.

"I'm happy."

Her fingers paused in their ministrations as she started massaging my scalp. I could hear the smile in her voice when she replied, "I'm glad you're happy with me."

"Why's that?"

"Well..." she paused, uncertain with her words as her fingers paused ever so briefly as they combed through my hair. "I kind of hoped you might let me stay with you."

The growl in my chest increased, and Misha laughed. But her smile faded as I spun around, and my brows drew together. "What about your friends?"

Her laughter ended, and her beautiful, bright eyes swam with uncertainty as she looked away from me. I lifted myself into a kneeling position, grabbed her chin, and tilted her head so she was forced to look at me. When her eyes eventually followed the movement to look at my face, the uncertainty had been replaced with determination, her jaw set and firm.

"Why haven't you asked about your friends?" I had been selfish in not asking her earlier, the guilt eating me up inside since, for the first time, I had strayed from my duty. Because my thoughts were not with protecting a misplaced species but protecting only *her.* Yet it seemed Misha had also been avoiding the topic, and I needed to know why.

"I don't want to find them." Her tone was firm, but the slightest tremble in her jaw betrayed her, along with the quickest shift of her gaze from mine to the side and back again.

"You're not being honest with me, Misha."

"So what?" she demanded and brushed my fingers from her chin. "We barely know each other. I don't have to tell you everything."

Her words hurt, and I couldn't explain why. My expression must have betrayed me as her eyes softened when she looked back at me, and her shoulders dropped as she sighed. "You say you want to stay with me, then you push me away. I don't understand. Did I do something wrong?"

She was an alien here and undoubtedly had customs I wasn't aware of. Were they a solitary species? Certain creatures in the ocean would fight if they got too close to each other and only reunited once every three years to mate. Were humans the same?

"You did nothing wrong, Sahcor."

The energy had drained from her voice, and I didn't like it. I preferred it when she was feisty, laughing, snapping a comeback at me, or when we had engaged in a real conversation, putting together clues and letting our minds work together as one. But I didn't approve of this tone. This tone felt like she had given up, but what she was giving up on I didn't understand.

Misha patted me on the shoulders, indicating I should sit again. I did but continued to face her, looking up into her eyes as she worked her fingers through my hair again. Her eyes were on me, but her mind was somewhere else.

"I told you the Ghaal tried to use me to find my friends," Misha said while she guided me to lean backward to dunk my hair. I did so, but when I sat up again, she continued massaging my scalp, almost as if she wasn't even aware she was doing it. I let her, not inclined to discourage her from touching me when it's all I could think about. "If I find the other girls, I'm afraid the Ghaal will somehow be following or tracking me. I don't want to endanger my friends, so it's best if I keep my distance."

"So, you resign yourself to a life without them to save them?"

Her fingers stopped moving in my hair, and her faraway gaze became focused as she looked at my face. "Why do you sound surprised? It's the same as what you did, isn't it?"

It was. It was almost exactly the same. I would have liked to live with my brothers, but we simply couldn't for our sanity and the sake of the abducted species. Designed to breed, if we were left alone together for too long, eventually half of us would change gender into female so breeding could commence. While we were in the lab, trying to prevent the change from being so close together was torture. Lanir was the first to begin the change, the scent of female hormones emanating from him enough to set off a chain reaction. I know he never forgave himself for being the first, seeing it as a sign of weakness, but none of us blamed him.

I suddenly wondered if I'd ever told him that and if I'd ever get another chance. Lanir fought hard and long, and the Ghaal tortured him worse than the rest of us from the moment he had showed signs of changing.

Vitri became mad with lust, lunging at Lanir, and Eldich wasn't far behind. I remember the whites of his eyes becoming dominant as they rolled back in his head as he strained against the change. I remember when I sensed the first tingling in my nostrils of female hormones from Eldich and felt my own urges rile up to take him, to mate.

Lanir was no weaker than the rest of us. We were all prisoners of our DNA.

I was never one to talk much, although now I wished I had told him these things. Perhaps he wouldn't have fled from us the moment we escaped, desperate to put as much distance as possible between him and us.

We were so determined not to help the Ghaal in the continuation of their species that we split up.

Now, Misha was doing the same, sacrificing her chance at being with her kind to save them.

I found myself torn again. Perhaps if we all got together—my brothers and the other human females—we could keep each other safe, and Misha wouldn't have to worry. Then she would have her family back, and I would have mine. Together, we'd have a new family.

Yet I didn't want to bring this up with Misha now. She was internally battling her thoughts, a struggle I knew too well and would need some time. I'd give her time, and then we could discuss finding her friends again.

As long as I didn't have to let her go.

A growl rumbled through my chest as Misha threaded her fingers through my hair again. She hummed gently, her eyes unfocused, but inside, she was far away from here, and I wondered where she went in her mind. My cock jerked to life when I focused on her breasts, still dappled with the droplets of water from the stream and shifting gently in front of my face, mesmerizing me. They shifted again when she chuckled, and I looked up to find her staring down at me, a small smile playing on her lips.

"You are so beautiful, Misha." I'd told her before, and I'd tell her repeatedly until she realized what I saw in her. With every passing moment, it became clearer to me how selfless and intelligent she was. She was an incredible female, and, of course, I couldn't help but desire her. On top of these feelings I didn't know I was capable of, was my instinct to mate. Together, it created a potent cocktail of pheromones, chemicals, and lust, and I gently raised my hands and placed them on her naked hips.

Misha didn't stop me from touching her, but her body's response was to shimmy her hips slightly in my light grip as if my touch wasn't where she really wanted it.

"You're not so bad yourself," she whispered, her voice husky with lust. My cock twitched again.

"You don't find me repulsive?"

Another light chuckle and mesmerizing movement of her breasts. "We're different, but you excite me, Sahcor, even if I feel like admitting that is wrong."

"Wrong, how?" I couldn't wait any longer and raised my hands to cup her breasts, placing my thumbs over her nipples. I was rewarded with a gasp from Misha and a shudder down her spine.

"We're different species and shouldn't feel this way. Like I shouldn't *want* you to touch me." She sighed as I massaged her breasts. "Your pheromones you told me about, are they affecting my judgment?"

I shook my head, careful to keep my eyes ahead so I didn't lose a moment of how her dappled skin looked encased in my hands. "They increase any existing attraction, but the pheromones are not a drug."

"Any existing attraction..." she whispered so quietly. I glanced up at her face in time to see her close her eyes as she arched her back, pushing her breasts into my touch. Pulling Misha toward me, I wrapped my lips around one of her nipples and flicked my tongue over the hardening bud. She gasped again, and her hands came to rest on my shoulders.

When I gave the same attention to the other nipple, I was drunk on the sounds she was making, keening and whimpering as she pushed herself closer to me. Just as abruptly as we'd started, Misha pulled away, and I snarled at her, gripping her hips and yanking her closer. Her laugh was breathless, and when I looked up, her green eyes were hooded with pleasure.

"Stand up," she instructed, and I did, the water sloshing around me, and my erection brushed against her stomach as I rose. Misha grabbed one of the root berries and squeezed the oil onto her hands, and before I could ask what she was doing, she wrapped her hands around my cock and started stroking me, and my knees almost buckled.

CHAPTER 14

MISHA

Taking my time, I felt every bump on his cock, inspecting the shape of it with my fingers. Sahcor didn't take his eyes from me, his gaze glued to where my hands wrapped around his cock, and I smiled, marveling at how I could make him come undone with a simple touch.

Sahcor had told me his pheromones didn't drug me and couldn't affect my judgment or make me do anything I didn't want to do, and I believed him. Because I was already attracted to him, and despite his size and strength, I wasn't afraid of him. In fact, I felt *I* held the power here, the way he trembled under my touch, the near-constant growl that emanated from his chest, and his insistent grip on my upper arms as though he was trying to hold back from thrusting into my palm.

The feeling had come over me so quickly I decided not to question it. I wanted Sahcor. I did. I wanted to touch every inch of him and explore his alien body. I wanted to know if the gills on his neck were sensitive, and if I brushed my lips across them while I rode him, would he come harder? There was trust and companionship with him, the type that can only be formed by going through something together. He had risked his life to save me, and I could see no point in further denying myself the desire to touch him.

To be fucked by him.

A shudder ran down my spine at the thought, and I could see a question forming behind Sahcor's lips at the way he glanced at me. To silence him, I worked his cock harder, used both hands to encompass his impressive length, and twisted them for extra stimulation. The oil worked so well on his skin, making him slippery and even smoother than he already was. His cock was the same gray color as his body, with a simple dapple of neon-purple spots running up the side and over his head. It was bumpy at the base, but the length was smooth and long, and I wanted to run my tongue over those purple markings.

I wanted to see his face as I did it.

"Misha," Sahcor moaned, jutting his hips forward into my hands. "I need to taste your cunt."

My knees weakened at his words, and my hands lost their rhythm. No one had ever spoken to me like that before. It was so primal, and I clenched my legs together.

"Okay," I whispered.

Sahcor moved quickly, and I squealed in surprise as he grabbed my waist, lifted me, and laid me down on the bank of the stream. His hands were between my legs and grabbed my thighs to spread them wide. A rush of cool air hit my pussy, and I trembled as Sahcor groaned, the unworldly sound running through his chest. He said something in a language I didn't understand before he kneeled between my legs and inhaled deeply.

His breath tickled, and I laughed as I squirmed under his touch. Sahcor placed a hand on my stomach and held me still as his eyes met mine over my body. "Do you want me to touch you, Misha?"

I didn't hesitate. "I want everything with you, Sahcor."

He dived forward and plunged his tongue into my pussy. His tongue was smooth and rubbery, and immediately, I lurched forward, grabbed his hair, and twisted it in my fingers as a moan was pulled from my throat. It was like being fucked with a dildo, and his nose rubbed against my clit, the heated huff of his breath against me as he growled and devoured me. I ground against his face shamelessly, not realizing how much I needed release until he started touching me.

Not realizing how much I'd been denying my attraction to him.

I laid back as Sahcor fucked me with his tongue, unable to stop myself from twisting and twitching under his ministrations. The slick muscle of his tongue moved in and out of me, and I clenched around him, needing *more*. As I reached down to rub my clit, Sahcor's bright eyes followed the movement of my hand, and he let me touch myself as his tongue stayed buried inside me.

Sahcor pulled back, and I almost whimpered from the loss of sensation.

"What are you doing?" he asked, his voice husky as he watched, hypnotized as my fingers rubbed my clit in small circles.

"Touching my clit." There was something so intimate about the fascination with which he watched me touch myself, and his eyes darkened as his tongue darted out to lick my juices from his lips. "It'll make me come."

"I want to touch it." It was a demand, and immediately, I withdrew my hand from between my legs. Sahcor's fingers traced their way up my thighs, and when he touched my clit with his thumb, he pressed *hard*, and my hips bucked toward him. A satisfied growl came from him, louder than I'd heard it before, and he leaned forward and pressed his tongue against the bundle of nerves before he licked at it madly. It was firm, wet, and intense, and I began writhing again, barely aware of the soft grasses crushed beneath my body.

"Fuck, *fuck,* Sahcor. I'm going to come..." He didn't stop, but the growling increased. I gripped his hair, and my legs clamped closed around his head as my orgasm shuddered through me. Sahcor kept going as my hips bucked against the contact until I used his hair to pull him away from my pussy. "Too much, it's too much. You can stop now."

When his gaze met mine, his pupils were blown out with lust, and he licked his lips again. "I never want to stop tasting you."

"Fuck," I muttered and pushed myself up to sit. I grabbed his head, pulled him toward me, and pressed my lips to his. When he opened his mouth in a gasp, I sucked on his tongue, tasting my arousal on him. Sahcor groaned as his arms came around me. The growling never stopped, and the brush of his erect cock against my thigh as he rocked his hips against me.

When he pulled away, his lip lifted into a smirk. "You surprise me, my mate."

"Why? What did I do?" I panted. I wanted *more.*

I couldn't believe that of all the times he chose to be chatty, it was *now.*

"What was that?"

"What was…" Realization hit me, and I grabbed his cheeks. "Have you never kissed before?" Sahcor shook his head as much as he could in my grip, his brows drawing together as I chuckled. "Damn, I just assumed with the way you went down on me, how you were using your tongue…"

"I was fucking your cunt with my tongue to taste you." I moaned at the way he said it, so matter-of-fact, as if I hadn't just orgasmed on his face. "Do you want me to fuck your mouth with my tongue too? I'd like to try it."

I tugged his hair lightly. "So try it."

Sahcor responded enthusiastically and mirrored my grip on his face before he pulled me toward him. He plunged his tongue into my mouth and proceeded to fuck it in and out past my lips. I coaxed him with my tongue, encouraging him, and circled them together before I nipped at his lips until he slowed down. The moment slowed and stretched out over minutes as we tasted each other. He tasted like the ocean, earthy and masculine. His pheromones filled the air between us and mixed with the tang of the sea air, and his movements slowed to a leisurely crawl. The waves crashed over the rocks where the edge of the peninsula met the water, and I could get lost in his taste and feel.

I opened my eyes to find Sahcor staring at me, and I smiled as he withdrew his tongue.

"Fuck me, Sahcor," I whispered, more emboldened by the minute with how he looked at me and seemed to worship every part of me.

Sahcor stepped back as I stood and turned, and I pushed myself onto my toes to rub his erection against my ass. He groaned, and his fingers gripped my waist, the webbing between his fingers cool against my skin. Shifting up slightly, I bent over the bank of the stream, and this time, Sahcor snarled and gripped me. I expected him to ask again if I wanted him and *this*—as if bending over in front of him and grinding against his cock wasn't clear enough—but there had been a shift in his demeanor, and whatever inclination he'd had before to talk had vanished. When I turned to meet his eyes, the green was blazing bright, and the animal was showing through as he shifted to line up his cock against my pussy.

I was dripping wet already, and the feel of the smooth head of his cock breaching me pulled a guttural moan I couldn't help. I fisted the grass on the bank, pulling up several bunches as he pushed in slowly and forced me to stretch around him. On instinct, I widened my legs, trying to ease the pressure as my body rebelled against the intrusion, telling me I was *too full!*

"Ahh..." I whimpered as I stretched around him, thankful I was wet enough to help ease him inside. I imagined this was what it was like to be fisted, and the mental image that slapped me across the face brought another groan from my lips.

But when he pulled out just as slowly before pushing in again, pleasure flared inside me, and I moaned again. He repeated the motion, and I could feel his body trembling behind me as he maintained the slow and steady pace. My leg started to shake, and I dropped my body forward onto the bank as he slipped fully inside, bottoming out.

"Fuck, Sahcor, that feels so good..."

He simply groaned in response, the near-constant growl a background noise to the sounds of the stream splashing around his legs as he began thrusting harder into me and gripped my hips to hold me in place. I turned my head, eager to watch him as he fucked me. Sahcor's eyes were closed, his face tilted to the sky, and the sun played off the neon-purple pattern on his skin. I took in the lines of his chest and the tautness of the muscles in his arms as he drove into me.

We were so different. He was an *alien,* and there was something so deliciously taboo about that knowledge that my pussy clenched around him. But the shape of him was so familiar, beyond the color and texture of his skin, and I hungrily eyed his chest and abs as he tilted my hips up to fuck me harder.

There must be something wrong with me. My eyes fluttered, but I couldn't stop staring. *But I'm too cock drunk right now to give a fuck.*

Sahcor's eyes flew open as I clenched on him again, and he met my gaze but didn't stop in his thrusts. Every push forced me open further, and the soil around my stomach became muddy as water splashed about me.

I'll need another bath.

Oh nooo. Sahcor will need to wash me again. What a shame.

"Come for me, Misha," Sahcor growled out. He shifted to grip my shoulders and push in a bit deeper when I thought it wasn't possible and forced a grunt past my lips.

"Fuck," I whispered, my pussy clenched desperately around his cock. Even with the bumpy texture around the base of his cock hitting all the right spots, it wasn't enough. "I can't. I need to touch my clit."

When he leaned over my body, his hips still snapping against my ass and thighs, I felt his grip tighten on my shoulders as his breath came hot against my neck. The weight of him pushed me further into the mud, and I gasped as my cheek was pressed against the ground. "I guess I'll just need to make it up to you by tongue fucking your cunt again."

My eyes rolled back into my head as Sahcor straightened. His fingers pressed bruises into my hips as he fucked me mercilessly, and each thrust caused me to cry out with pleasure. I didn't want him to stop. I wanted him to keep fucking me like this forever. The freedom of it, the secret pleasure just between us, the breaking down of expectations, and anything I ever dreamed of as an *alien* fucked me—it felt *so fucking good.* The sounds of nature hadn't stopped, and they reminded me we were exposed here, outdoors, yet somehow still in our private little place.

Away from any troubles, from anyone, and from the Ghaal.

Just him and me, and the pleasure we gave each other with absolute primal need.

I needed nothing else.

Sahcor roared as he came and pressed deep into me. The rush of cum was hot and thick, and I could feel it forced out of my pussy around his cock by the sheer volume of it. I slumped and barely had a moment to suck in a gasping breath before Sahcor flipped me onto my back and forced my thighs open. Pushing myself up on my elbows, I watched, slack-jawed, as he used two of his large fingers to scoop up his cum and push it back inside me. When he was satisfied, and the growl in his chest had eased to a comfortable rumble, he tapped at my sensitive clit, and as my hips bucked, a dangerous smile played on his lips.

"I'm going to lick and suck your clit, Misha..." he said as my eyes widened, "... and make sure your cum is all over my face until you're limp in my arms, then I'll bathe you again."

"Uh-huh." I couldn't think straight, and my leg jerked as he tapped again on my clit.

"Then I'm going to make you come again."

"Okay," I whispered, the word ending in a gasp as his lips found my clit.

What else can I say to that?

CHAPTER 15

MISHA

Sahcor and I lazed about most of the day. As I drifted on my back in the narrow stream, my eyes closed against the onslaught of the sun, I realized how long it had been since I'd done this. While it didn't soothe the reality I wouldn't be going home, it was a golden nugget I could cling to. We splashed about in the water, snacking on the sweet root berries from the grasses that seemed to grow in abundance, and fucked more than once. It was like a strange dream, where I was having fun and relaxing, but there was that constant undercurrent of danger I couldn't run from—a vibration through the air that never settled or let me forget the Ghaal was out there.

And they were after me.

With little grace, I dropped my knees to the base of the stream and shuffled toward Sahcor across the mossy base. He offered me a berry, and without thinking, I opened my mouth rather than taking it with my fingers. He paused, and as always, he seemed to assess every situation before he acted. When he placed the berry in my mouth, his fingers danced a small trail across my bottom lip, and I hummed.

I wiped my mouth with the back of my hand, and Sahcor snatched my wrist, turning my hand over and investigating my fingers. "What's wrong with your hands?"

"What?" I checked to see what he was looking at, and the familiar rippling of the skin on my fingertips hit the light as he turned my hand back and forth, and concern pulled his eyebrows together. "Oh, that. That happens when we're in the water for a long time."

"Why?"

I shrugged. "A leftover from evolution, I think. Used to help us grip underwater or something, or so I've been told."

"You're evolving to survive in the water, like me?"

I chuckled quietly. "No, humans don't work

like that."

Sahcor seemed disappointed but smiled when he looked at me and pushed a strand of wet hair out of my face. His thumb brushed across my nose. "And what is the purpose of these spots?"

"Freckles."

"Another evolutionary trait?"

I laughed. "An evolutionary fail in my genes, I'm afraid. It's my skin's attempt to tan and, instead, it goes..." I made a raspberry with my lips and splayed my fingers out in an explosion motion, "... and spits out a tiny dot of pigment. A freckle."

"I like them." Sahcor dotted his finger against my nose a few times, touching several freckles.

Smiling, I said, "Me too." I didn't particularly like them about me before. But with the way Sahcor stared at them with fascination, as if every part of me—including any imperfections I would normally cover with makeup—were something to behold, I liked that *he* liked them. I liked this alien man and how he made me feel comfortable even in a highly uncomfortable situation. He'd done more than save me—he'd welcomed me into his home, fed and cared for me. He treated me as more than a guest, but as a friend right from the beginning when he had no reason to trust me or even care. I understood there was something going on underneath the surface, an instinct he couldn't control and a desire to mate. But the thing was—he didn't *have* to be nice about it. Sahcor could be an animal and simply take what he wanted from me. He was more than strong enough to overpower me.

But he didn't. He *wouldn't.*

The shiver that ran down my spine at the realization of my growing feelings for this being had nothing to do with the chill as the late afternoon air changed. But Sahcor ran his hands up and down my arms. "We should get back to the cave, and I'll make you some clothes and get us some fish."

"It's a date." I chuckled at his quizzical expression, but before he could ask, I lifted myself from the stream, immediately chilled as the winds hit my wet skin. "Fuck me," I muttered and bent down to pick up my clothes.

The air was knocked from my lungs as I was tackled, and I rolled in the grass as Sahcor landed on top of me while one of his large hands spread my thighs apart before he pumped his cock a few times. Immediately, I was dripping wet for him, the lingering memory of him inside me enough to make me wet.

"Whoa, whoa, Sahcor, wait up." I tried to slow my breathing after the surge of adrenaline.

He paused and lifted his blazing eyes to mine. "Misha?"

"What are you doing?" The head of his cock was rubbing against my pussy, and I was finding it difficult to concentrate. My teeth started to chatter, and the cold winds seemed to increase in strength with every passing minute. The heat of Sahcor was on top of me, surrounding me, but it wasn't enough to battle against my wet extremities and the coolness of the soil underneath the grass.

"You asked me to fuck you."

He started pushing the head of his cock into my pussy, and I moaned, ready for him.

This *should not* turn me on as much as it did.

It should not!

It should not!

I shook my head, trying to figure out what caused the confusion while I fought the urge to roll my eyes back in my head as he continued to penetrate me.

Fuck me.

I huffed out a breathless laugh and placed my hands against his chest. "It's just an expression. I'm sorry, the coldness of the wind startled me."

His eyes sought answers in mine, and he froze. "Do you wish me to stop?"

I couldn't help my body responding to him, and my hips jerked upward, seeking further stimulation as his cock entered me. We moaned together, and I wrapped my arms around his shoulders. I was cold, wet, and hungry, and we *really* should get back to Sahcor's cave.

But as he sunk in farther...

"Fuck..." I hissed the word out even as I gritted my teeth against the chatter. "Fuck me hard and fast, Sahcor, and then we'll go back to the cave."

Sahcor responded with a single hard thrust that buried him deep inside me. We'd fucked a few times today, and not once had we done it in missionary. But *fuck,* I wished we had. The bumps around the base of his cock hit my clit just right this way, and if I ground my hips upward to meet his movements, I might just be able to come like this. I shuddered, my body already preparing for the impending pleasure.

My attention returned to Sahcor when he dragged his fingertips down my cheek, and I met his eyes. "So beautiful, Misha," he muttered, and I clenched around him at the words. He was dragging his cock in and out of me at an agonizingly slow pace, and I wanted *more.* The growling in his chest vibrated against my sensitive nipples, and when I began twitching as my orgasm drew near, he only held me tighter.

I wrapped my legs around his waist as he drove into me and gripped his shoulders. "Sahcor," I said, grabbing his hair and yanking it gently to get his attention. His growling spiked at the harsh treatment, and his eyes blazed. "Fuck me," I said as I held his eye contact. "Hard. And. Fast."

He snarled and grabbed my hair the same way I had his, tilted my head back, and pounded into me until all I could do was hold onto him as I came around his cock.

The winds howled through the maze of rocks as we returned to Sahcor's cave. Once deep enough within the cave system, the sound of the winds was drowned out, and I flopped gratefully onto the bed of dried seaweed and rubbed my feet.

"Is it like that every night?" I asked Sahcor as he kneeled near me and drew out longer strands of the seaweed from the bedding before putting them aside. "The winds?"

"Yes, although sometimes it's raining and storming as well. The winds alone are tame."

"They didn't seem tame," I huffed and ran my fingers through my hair, trying to detangle it enough to braid it. It was fine after washing it with the oils until we had to walk back to the cave, and the winds whipped it around something fierce. "Can I have one of those? Just a little one."

Sahcor handed me a small strip, and once I had braided my hair, I tied the end by twisting the seaweed around it and tugged slightly on it before nodding my approval. It would certainly help not to have my hair getting knotty every five seconds. When Sahcor glanced at me, he released an angry grunt. "You didn't need to put your old clothes back on."

"Okay, well, for one, I'm not leaving my favorite pajamas in the middle of nowhere, no matter how tatty they are. And two, I'm also not walking through a narrow cave naked. I'd rather my boobs and butt don't get all scuffed up, thank you."

He grunted again, but the smallest lift of his lip betrayed him, and I chuckled.

Kneeling next to him, I helped him sort through some weeds. "I'm sorry we're having to steal from your bedding to make clothes. I can use these for a little while if you need to wait."

Sahcor handed me a bundle of weeds. "I'll get some more to dry tomorrow to replace the bedding. You need clothes."

"Can I help make them?"

"Okay."

I'm not sure why, but I started to glance around to see what he might use to put my new clothes together. Don't get me wrong, I wasn't expecting to find a sewing machine or anything, but just *something,* maybe some bone needles and thread of some kind. Really anything because right now, I couldn't imagine how he would turn the weeds in my hands into clothes.

"It won't be much," he said as he moved to a better-lit area in the cave, taking advantage of the light that came through the bright crystals. "But it'll at least cover your..." his eyes did a once-over of my body, "... boobs and butt." His lip lifted again, exposing his sharp teeth as he looked down. "Although I'd rather if you stayed naked." The last part was delivered as a rushed mutter, and when I chuckled, he glanced at me from the corner of his eye, lifting one eyebrow as if to check if I'd heard.

I sat next to him. "I'm sure you would, but we can't stay naked and fuck all day."

"Why not?"

"Because we need to..."

What?

Because we need to *what, Misha?*

I had no job to go to, no errands to run, no bills to pay, or phone calls to make. I had absolutely zero responsibilities here except to stay safe and alive. Sahcor had told me about his brothers and how they would have worked to get to the other girls and keep them safe. I had landed closest to the colony anyway, and Sahcor assured me he would keep an eye on the colony. Apparently, he was quite adept at moving around the village at night, and he'd make sure the others weren't taken.

All we really had to do was get food, bathe, and sleep.

And *fuck.*

We *needed* to stay away from the Ghaal, and I *needed* to keep away from the girls for their safety.

But beyond that, our only needs were survival and pleasure.

I didn't pick up my sentence after trailing off, and Sahcor and I fell into a comfortable silence. He would watch me as if figuring me out until I could almost hear the cogs in his mind turning. He'd put things together and make assumptions about life on Earth and the life I came from with what little I'd told him today. I'd tell him *all* about it one day—it's not like we didn't have the time. But today, it was simply nice not to think for a moment, and while I wasn't one hundred percent relaxed, I could at least let myself recover mentally from the past few weeks.

While Sahcor watched me, I shamelessly checked him out and allowed my gaze to wander from where his damp hair fell across his shoulders, over his chest and arms, and down to where his cock lay against his thigh.

When I realized I was staring, my gaze jumped back to his face. There was no judgment in his expression and perhaps a hint of a smile.

"Do you wish to fuck, Misha?"

Oh, so formal. My pussy clenched at his words, but I was a bit tender. Sahcor wasn't small, and we'd already had a lot of fun today. I licked my lips, suddenly desperate for some water.

Or a vodka.

"Later. I'm a bit tender."

The hint of the smile dropped from his face at the same time he dropped the weeds so he could reach up and cup my face in both his hands. "Did I hurt you?"

Placing my hands over his, I smiled. "No, no. But you're so... big."

"Your cunt was so tight around my cock."

Fuck, maybe we shouldn't do anything but stay naked and fuck all day.

This wasn't me. I wasn't a sex kitten always ready to go, but Sahcor brought this out of me. It was the ultimate release and surrender. I was stuck here on this planet, and somehow, I'd wound up being rescued by a sexy-as-fuck alien who wanted *me.* I simply nodded at his words and bit my lip again. "Mm-hmm," I agreed and leaned into his touch.

"I will lick your cunt better tonight, Misha, after I have fed you."

"Okay," I whispered, the memory of his rubbery tongue sliding into my pussy so vivid I clenched around nothing.

I guess there were things to look forward to on this planet.

CHAPTER 16

SAHCOR

"Watch again." I repeated the action of weaving the dried seaweed strands together. Misha leaned over me this time and placed a hand on my thigh to steady herself as she watched my motions with her tongue sticking slightly out. It was adorable, and I tried to ignore the feel of her fingers so close to my cock. I was meant to be teaching her how to weave, but she was getting frustrated.

"Look, crafts just aren't my strong suit." She sat back as she lifted then dropped her previous tangled attempts.

"It's okay, you'll learn. I'll finish this, and then I'll

get you something to eat. You've only had berries all day."

"Are they not good for you?"

"They're fine, but they're not substantial enough for a meal and don't have many nutrients."

Misha's brows drew together. "Shit, I'm sorry, Sahcor. We could've left the stream and gotten something better to eat. I don't want you to go hungry."

"I didn't want to leave the stream."

She met my gaze, and my fingers paused because I was sure she knew what I was thinking. I'd thought of little else since she first wrapped her small fingers around my cock and invited me to fuck her. The feel of her was nothing short of incredible, and while I had to push harder than I would have liked to get her cunt to open up and accept my cock, Misha liked it. I'd held back until we were about to head home when she'd told me to fuck her *hard and fast.*

Her little cunt opened up to me, and the harder I fucked her, the more of those delicious noises she made until she was coming around my cock. She squeezed me until I had nothing left to give and milked my seed from me. Now I knew she liked it harder, I could fuck her harder.

Although I did enjoy the way her brow pulled together in frustration when I went slow, and her hips bucked toward me as she tried to get me in deeper, sooner.

My Misha was insatiable.

Her gaze dropped to my lap again as my cock twitched to life, hardening and straightening. Misha gasped, and I groaned. "You're not helping my concentration," I grumbled out.

"Me?" She slapped a hand to her chest. "I didn't even *do* anything. You were the one having dirty thoughts."

A growl rumbled through my chest, and my hands trembled where I held the weave I'd started. "You were thinking about my cock inside you, too, Misha. I can smell your arousal."

"Well... I... that's just..." She stammered her way through several responses before she lunged forward and grabbed my cock. My cry of surprise ended in a deep growl as I dropped my work and grabbed her wrist.

"What are you doing?"

She grinned. "*Really* distracting you."

MISHA

Sahcor's gaze was pinned to his lap, where my fingers wrapped around his smooth cock as I languidly pumped up and down. When he met my eyes, there was a glint in them I hadn't seen before. "Do you want to play this game?" he asked, an undercurrent of danger in his tone that made me shudder with excitement. Was Sahcor *kinky?* I'd never done anything particularly kinky before, if you exclude sex with a sea alien, that is. My excitement was interrupted by a ripple of hesitation. Somehow, I seemed to forget that Sahcor was an *alien,* and what if kinky to him was... I wouldn't even know where to go with that. What if it was something I wouldn't even consider or something I wasn't physically *capable* of?

Sahcor's teeth, slightly sharper than I'd been expecting the first time I saw him smile, were exposed when he grinned and stared at me from under his brow. He dropped the weaving he was working on in one motion, stood, grabbed my arms, and pulled me to my feet with him. He draped my arms around his neck, and I intertwined my fingers, standing on my toes and tilting my head up, ready for a kiss that never came.

I shuddered when he leaned down and brushed his lips past my ear.

"Deep breath, Misha."

"Wha—"

Screaming, I gripped my legs around Sahcor as he dove into the water, his movements completely unhindered by my body wrapped around the front of his. When we surfaced outside the cave, I gasped and spluttered, and Sahcor laughed. "Do I have to tell you again?"

"I... just..." I coughed and glared at him as we bobbed in the ocean. The water was churning around us, splashing menacingly against the rocks outside the hidden cave. Sahcor remained unmoving, but I'm certain without him, I'd be smashed against them. "Just give me a second."

He watched me, the grin never leaving his face while I steadied my breathing and took a few deep breaths. I nodded at him, and Sahcor waited until I'd sucked in a lungful of air before he dove again. Tucking my head against Sahcor's chest, I did my best to keep myself calm. He didn't seem to be diving deep, and while the water was calmer underneath, it was dark and cold.

We stopped after only a few seconds. I tried opening my eyes underwater, but the image was blurry. Sahcor's form was in front of me after he unwrapped my limbs from around his body, his eyes bright. But with the purple markings on his skin, I had to internalize my gasp. They *glowed* underwater, and he looked nothing short of magnificent. Sahcor was holding my upper arms, and as he moved his hands away, I shook my head vigorously and gripped his wrists. There was a sound that could have been a chuckle from him, muffled by the press of the ocean around us.

I looked up, the water sending the light from the moon into a rippling mess. I'd guess we were less than a foot from the surface. This comforted me, and I moved my gaze back to Sahcor. He dropped a hand lower, gripping and massaging my breast, his other hand keeping a firm grip on my upper arm. After flicking my nipple, he chuckled again as I glared at him, unable to gasp, moan, or make any sound for fear of losing air. His smooth hand moved between my legs, and he deftly pushed a finger inside me, his thumb finding my clit and rubbing. My nails dug into his arm as he worked me, pumping his thick finger in and out.

My head started to spin, my mind screaming at me to get air. I gripped Sahcor's bicep and used my other hand to point upward, but he simply kept working my pussy, and the pleasure was mixing with the panic. When I tried to swim away, Sahcor wrapped an arm around my waist and held me still as he forced my body closer to orgasm.

As I came, I threw my head back, screaming as we burst through the water's surface after a powerful kick from Sahcor's muscular legs. He held me as I gasped for air, my legs shaking through my orgasm.

"Who's distracting who now?"

"That's not fair..." I gasped out, trying to catch my breath. "I can't swim like you can. I can't... I can't..." I waved my hands about, "... simply *pick you up* and throw you in the ocean."

Sahcor chuckled. "Your little cunt sucked my fingers in so nicely, I think you came hard."

"Well, yes…" I huffed out an impatient breath. "But I could've died."

His grin dropped. "I would never let anything hurt you."

I huffed an amused breath through my nose before I sighed loudly and swiped my hand through my hair. "You're unbelievable."

"You don't believe me?"

This time, I laughed. "I mean… you're incredible."

Sahcor tilted his head slightly as he smiled at me, his wet hair plastered to his face and neck. We bobbed in the water for a while, the winds whipping around us and sending a shiver down my spine. We were at the mercy of the waves, and when I looked down, I could barely see the outline of Sahcor's legs pumping underwater, holding us both afloat.

Incredible.

"Hungry?" he asked.

My stomach chose that moment to grumble loudly. "Yes, please."

Sahcor hummed thoughtfully, gazing into the water below us. I wondered how much he could see in the murky depths, certainly more than I could.

"Unfortunately, it's too late for hacku. I'll have to get them for you another day." His eyes met mine. "Can you keep yourself afloat a moment while I dive, or would you rather come with me?"

Panic gripped my chest, and I tried not to show

it, although my teeth automatically sought out my lip and chewed in a nervous gesture I couldn't help. Glancing around, I couldn't see *anything*—not the cave where we had come from, the rocks, the shore, or any signs of life. Heavy waves lifted me up and down in a motion that was soothing with Sahcor, and terrifying without him. The darkness was overwhelming. I'd been swimming at night before, but even on Earth, I wouldn't venture out to sea this far at any time of the day or night. Alone or not.

"I..."

Underwater, Sahcor grabbed my hand and guided it to his shoulder. "Hold on."

Trust. I had absolute and pure trust in this being, this *alien*—more than I had ever trusted anyone. It's one thing to say of someone *I would trust them with my life,* but with Sahcor, I did, and he'd proven himself worthy of that trust over and over again.

When he smiled at me, his eyes caught the light glinting off the moon, enhancing everything alien about him and making him simply breathtaking.

"Hold tight."

SAHCOR

Surfacing as quickly as possible, I finished killing the fish underwater to save Misha the visual of beheading and cleaning our meal. Misha gasped as we surfaced, and I handed her a fish, running my tongue over my sharp teeth to make sure there were no entrails or blood lingering in my mouth. My female wasn't stupid and knew where meat came from, but she also admitted she hadn't been hunting before, not like I hunted. Without her needing to say anything, I decided I would ease her into my world and way of life. She didn't need to ask. I could read the lines on her face and the gestures her small hands made—her nervousness and uncertainty but also her happiness and arousal. She was an open book, and I'd like to think she was only this way with me.

We ate and chatted, and while Misha was kicking her thin legs with her webless toes, I kept an arm wrapped around her waist and took most of her weight, making sure to keep her head above the water. It was good for her to keep moving, though. The water was cold, and I hadn't intended on staying out this long at night.

Only enough to play a game with her after she teased me.

I was about to suggest we return to the cave after we finished eating when Misha asked, "How far can you see underwater when it's dark like this?"

"Far enough. The water is mostly clear, and I have decent enough night vision to keep safe."

She smiled and said, "Tell me what you see." She ducked underwater, and I followed, holding her hands as we hovered beneath the surface. The sounds of the violent winds were muted by the dull thud of the ocean's heartbeat as it moved around us.

Misha's eyes were open, and she looked around with her eyebrows drawn together. She wanted me to tell her what I could see, but all I could see was her. Her dark hair moved around her with the waves, washing back and forth across her face and neck with the motion of the water that would otherwise be invisible under the surface.

Her eyes widened, and she drew a hand to her mouth, following a movement behind my back. When she surfaced, I followed suit.

"I think I saw a school of fish!"

I couldn't help but smile at her enthusiasm. I hadn't felt the vibrations of something large, and most small fish moved with the water. "What did they look like?"

She reached out and touched the markings on my face. "Neon-purple dots, like across your skin, moving through the water."

My smile dropped. Hacku? At this time of night? It seemed so unlikely it bordered on impossible.

Which could only mean…

"Misha!" I grabbed for her a second too late, and she slipped through my fingers as her leg was snatched, and she was pulled underwater. I dove, my heart thumping so loud in my chest the sound echoed in my ears as the weight of water pressed around me, deeper and deeper into the ocean. Misha reached out for me, her arms outstretched, and dragged through the heavy rush of water that flowed around her as she was pulled downward. Her eyes were wide and fearful, and the purple glow of the maasi was visible below her, its jaws clenched around her leg.

My anger at myself for being complacent with Misha's safety drove me forward. The maasi were solitary hunters and wouldn't dare attack me. But Misha was smaller and more fragile, and her movements in the water betrayed her as being out of place. The maasi would have thought her injured or dying. The volti birds would often come out to sea at night to hunt, and the maasi used their purple-spotted coloring to trick them into thinking they were a school of fish, exactly as Misha had assumed. Once they got too close, the maasi would strike and drag them under until they drowned, then devour them.

My fingertips brushed Misha's briefly, and the fear in her eyes was exaggerated. Then, in that small moment, hope flared, only to be extinguished as her hand slipped from mine again.

It was too deep for the light from the moon to penetrate now, and I relied on my vision to get me closer. I could use the vibrations through the water, including the feel of Misha's form splashing about as she twisted. I panicked and tried to pull against the hold on her. However, that was drowned out by my panic because I knew Misha well enough to know the way she thrashed about would only be wearing her out.

She would run out of air soon.

With a surge of speed, I wrapped my fingers around Misha's wrist, tugged, and used my feet to bring myself to a stop and paddle back toward the surface. There was resistance, and when Misha's eyes screwed shut, there was a mist of red blood around her legs.

Refusing to let her go, I used my hold on her body to pull myself toward her feet, always keeping one hand latched firmly around her. When I reached the maasi, it stared at me, and its four wild purple eyes glowed. For a moment, I was thankful Misha couldn't see in the dark, for while I hated for her to be afraid, I didn't want her to see me at my most animal.

I lunged, sinking my teeth into the maasi's gills at the same time as I tugged Misha from its grip. Immediately, it let her go, the deep gray of its blood mixing with the color of Misha's and making the water murky. I didn't wait and thrust myself upward, Misha safely in my arms.

But not truly safe, not yet.

The panic was still in her eyes, and she clawed at her throat as she looked at me desperately. I couldn't move fast enough, and before we reached the surface, her eyes rolled back in her head, and her mouth opened as her body was desperate to get air. As she sucked in a lungful of water, her body spasmed and fought against me. Her body tried to correct the mistake by opening her mouth again and taking another doomed breath. I tried to stop her, but I needed to focus on getting to the surface.

When we broke through the waves, and the cool air whipped around my skin, Misha was unconscious in my arms.

The journey back to my cave took too long, even though we weren't far away. My entire body ached. I've never pushed myself harder to move faster through the water and keep up the speed.

Lifting Misha onto my cave's rocky floor, I hovered over her. "No, Misha, no, no." What should I do? I knew nothing about her anatomy. "Think, Sahcor, *think!*"

I was smarter than this, but I couldn't stop panicking. Every second she wasn't breathing was furthering the chance she wouldn't come back. Could she wake up at all? Grief and horror almost consumed me, and I moaned, squeezing her body against my chest as the sound reverberated around the cave.

Think, think, think!

"Misha, please help me... tell me what to do," I said, brushing my fingers over her body. "Help me, help me." With another roar that faded into a growl, I tried to control my panic.

Think, think, think!

"You're not a water being and don't have gills, so water in your lungs is a death sentence. I need to get the water out of your lungs."

I lifted her again and tilted her body before I slammed my palm against her back between her shoulder blades. This only made her lifeless limbs jolt.

Refusing to let panic win, I tried something crazy.

Pressing my mouth to hers, I pushed air from my lungs into hers and tried to force the water out.

Nothing.

I squeezed her and did it again.

When Misha coughed, my body slumped. I barely managed to keep enough control to hold her on her side, hitting her on the back again as she coughed up more water, and each time she dragged in a large and shuddering breath. She coughed up more water, vomited, and then coughed again, her entire body heaving with the effort. Misha was shaking and shuddering, her face pale, and her arms weakly flailed as she tried to understand what was happening and why she was in pain.

"Get it all up, Misha. Keep coughing."

There was another heavy intake of breath and more coughing.

Misha then went limp in my arms, and her eyes fluttered open. Her hand twitched as if she were going to try to lift it. "Sahcor…"

Then she passed out again, and for the first time in my life, I cried, holding her close so I could feel her breathing and steady heart.

MISHA

My entire body ached, and my head throbbed, but the worst pain was in my chest. It was like every muscle had been used to its limit and was protesting all at once.

Where was I?

My eyelids were heavy, but there were streaks of light burning against them and the heat of a body against mine.

The sensation of being grabbed around the leg and tugged underwater rushed back to the forefront of my mind—the crushing depth of the water, the darkness, and the sting of pain as teeth penetrated my skin.

Panicking, I sat and thrashed my arms about, desperate to get to the water's surface I was no longer underneath. Sahcor cried out and growled as my hand connected with his face, and when he grabbed my wrists to pin me down, I continued to writhe.

"Misha, it's me. You're safe now. Please be calm."

Despite my heart thumping, adding to the existing discomfort in my chest, I tried to still and anchor myself to the bright green of Sahcor's eyes. Letting my gaze dance around, I took in my surroundings. I wasn't underwater—I was in Sahcor's cave in the dried seaweed bed. The water rippling around the underwater entrance was bright with sunlight, and the purple crystal flecks in the cave ceiling glittered and cast colors across Sahcor's already beautiful skin.

A deep breath raked through my body, and I swallowed against nothing. More pain, dry and scratching, and before I could try to talk, Sahcor handed me the water bag and helped me drink until I'd had my fill. The cool water soothed my throat and eased the ache in my chest and gut.

I took a few moments to ground myself, hating the panic in Sahcor's eyes as he watched me with concern. "What happened?" I croaked out.

"I'm sorry, Misha. I failed you." I didn't understand and simply shook my head at him, waiting for him to continue. "You were grabbed by a maasi and dragged underwater. I shouldn't have had you out there at night. I should have realized you were smaller than me and, therefore, they would see you as prey. I should have never let you go, I should hav—"

With a shaking hand, I reached up and pressed my fingertips to his lips, ceasing his apologies, and shook my head again. I didn't need an explanation of all the things he did or didn't do because I'm certain whatever he did was to help me. A throb of pain reminded me my leg was injured, and when I looked down, I saw it had been wrapped in dark leaves.

He had saved me and looked after me.

"Not your fault," I whispered as I indicated for more water.

His eyes shimmered with pain, and I cupped his smooth cheek in my palm. "I was too late saving you," he whispered, his voice an aching croak as I drank more. "Your lungs took in water, and you stopped breathing."

My brows drew together. I didn't remember that part. "You saved me?"

"I didn't know what to do." The growling in his chest had started again, a constant background rumble to our conversation as he fussed with my hair, brushing it from my face, and laying me back in bed. "I had to get the water out of your lungs."

"You did. I'm still here."

"I almost lost you."

"You *saved* me," I breathed out the words and caressed his cheek.

"I failed you as a mate, Misha. You should never have been in danger in the first place."

"Please, Sahcor." I couldn't stand the guilt in his voice nor the wavering of his tone when he relived the pain of almost losing me. He cared for me beyond the duty he had spoken of when we met. A handful of days, and he already cared.

But I did, too, didn't I? I had already begun to accept my life here on this planet but with *him.* I still didn't want to put the other girls in danger and was stubborn in my resolve to keep my distance and not try to find them, but with Sahcor, I had a chance at a life. How incredible that I should fall into the lap of a being who I connected with so quickly, bound by circumstance and held together by mutual compassion and care.

And perhaps even the beginnings of love.

Could I grow to love Sahcor? I thought I could. There were many things to learn, including the challenges of this planet and new life, but all of it seemed a little easier with Sahcor.

What then? What happened when I knew how to hunt and look after myself and my way around?

A family?

I had been so horrified at the idea of an alien

baby with the Ghaal, but I didn't feel like that with Sahcor. I've always firmly believed that someone's physical appearance—how attractive they appeared—was tightly wound in with their personality. You could be with the most attractive person in the world, and if they opened their mouth and were horrible, abruptly, they weren't so attractive anymore. So, here I was staring at Sahcor, not even really seeing the small frills on his neck that hid his gills when he was on the surface, nor the gray and purple of his skin, his overly large frame, and one finger too few on each hand. None of those elements alone seemed to cement in my mind because all I saw when I looked at him was *Sahcor.*

A friend and lover, and potentially more on this planet I now needed to call home.

I touched my belly, and Sahcor's eyes followed the movement. With his thumb and forefinger, he pressed it to my stomach. His gaze that had been so intently fixed on my face dropped out of focus for a moment. "You are not pregnant."

I chuckled. "I didn't think I was."

He tilted his head as though he was trying to follow my thought process because he got caught back up in his, and his lips turned down. "You almost died. I almost lost you."

"But I didn't. You didn't."

"It was too close."

I grabbed his hand which still hovered over my

stomach. "I imagine there are a lot of things on this planet that could be dangerous for me, but we'll figure it all out."

He snarled, and I was caught halfway between recoiling and wanting to smile. "I will keep you here."

I chuckled. "You can't keep me locked in a cave."

There was a flash of something across his eyes like that was *exactly* what he was thinking of doing. When his gaze traced my body, I followed the movement and moaned as I reached down to tug at the rags of my clothes. "Oh no, my favorite pajamas." There were barely more than a few shredded scraps of material left, discolored and worn.

"They are special to you?" Sahcor asked.

"Well, yeah." It felt silly, but outside the fact I'd had these pajamas for years and bought them because the horses on them looked like Charlie, they were now the *only* thing I had from Earth. The one remnant of a life I could never go back to. I bit my lip against the rising emotion. It would be foolish to keep a few rags, but I couldn't let them go either.

"Raise your arms."

I did as Sahcor asked without question, and he delicately slid what was left of my top over my head. When he indicated, I lifted my hips from the bed so he could follow suit with my pants. He handled the fabric with care as though it would fall apart at any second. When I was naked, I held Sahcor's eye contact as he folded my pajamas over in his hands and held them close to his chest. "I will find a way to preserve them for you, Misha, and I will finish making your new clothes."

I wanted to tell him it wasn't necessary, that they were practically rubbish at this point, and we should just discard them, but I couldn't. "Thank you," I whispered.

He placed a hand on my forehead. "Rest, my mate. I will gather food for us, and we will stay here all day."

Sahcor returned not only with fish but also some of the gladvin root berries and a few other plants I had no idea of the names. This time, when he made a fire, he threw the fish and the plants onto a flat stone and pushed them around with a stick until the plants wilted and the fish skin was crisp. My mouth watered at the fragrances that filled the cave, and when I moved to try and get closer to the fire, Sahcor lifted his head, snarled at me, and jabbed his finger back at the bed of weeds. He held this pose until I returned to lie down. I smirked at him, and the slightest twitch of his lip betrayed him.

"I think you like bossing me around," I said, adjusting so I was more in a sitting position and leaned on one arm, careful not to rub against my injured leg. My nakedness didn't bother me so much because Sahcor was naked, too, and I was comfortable around him. I still wanted clothes, but here in the cave, where it was only the two of us, it felt natural.

His lip lifted again, exposing sharp teeth. "You need to rest your leg."

"Yeah, yeah, yeah," I muttered, still smiling, and settled back to wait for Sahcor to serve the food since, evidently, I wasn't allowed to help this time.

Thankfully, I didn't have to wait long, and Sahcor dragged the stone closer to the bed, picked up pieces of food, and held them out to me. "I can feed myself," I said, trying to accept the piece of cooked fish he was offering. Sahcor said nothing and simply stared me down until I lowered my hand and opened my mouth dutifully. I knew he felt guilty for what happened last night, but I was here and alive. And if the last few weeks had taught me anything, it was to seize every moment.

The cooked fish melted in my mouth, and I hummed my appreciation. Sahcor tried to continue feeding me, and I shook my head. "No, you and I eat together." He held one of the strange plants, which could almost be a string bean if it weren't a mustard yellow. "Nope," I pushed his hand away. "You eat, then I eat, we take turns."

His stare was intense, but I held my ground, even though I couldn't keep the smile from my face. He was receding into silence again as he often did. But I knew now that behind his silences wasn't a sea monster but a deep thinker. He'd be having some internal debate with himself, probably overthinking things as much as I did. Finally, he took the plant into his mouth and ate it before he hastily grabbed another to offer me.

"See? That wasn't so tough." I ate the bean he offered, and since he wasn't in a talking mood, I continued, "You care for me, Sahcor, I understand that. Now, what you need to understand is that I care for you also. It makes me uncomfortable to sit here and eat while you aren't. I need to know you're getting fed too."

His only response was another tilt of the head and him eating a piece of fish without fighting me about it first. We finished the meal that way, Sahcor taking a bite himself after every piece he fed me. He was breaking off larger pieces for me, but I said nothing, figuring I had won the battle at least with making sure he was eating rather than waiting for me to finish like I was royalty or something.

Sahcor didn't complain when he helped me hobble off the bed so I could use the bathroom, and remained silent as he unwrapped the seaweed from my leg to replace it.

I hissed through the sting as he removed the weeds. The bite marks in my leg were deep, and I bit my lip as I studied them. At least they looked clean, but the skin was angry and red around the wounds. Is this the sort of thing I'd get stitches for back home? Antibiotics? I had none of that here and had to trust Sahcor knew what was best. "Are these the same plants you use for bedding?"

"No. Those have no nutritional value… these are medicinal." He dunked the ones he'd collected in the seawater before wrapping my leg again, the cool water soothing the pain slightly.

Sahcor wiped his thumb across my forehead as I lay down again. I hadn't realized I'd been sweating—my body's response to pain I was trying to pretend I didn't feel. "I'm sorry, Misha," he murmured.

"If you keep apologizing, I'm going to kick your ass."

His eyebrows furrowed. "For what purpose?"

I laughed. "Oh my God, Sahcor." I covered my mouth with the back of my hand, stifling the giggles that tumbled out. It wasn't *that* funny, but everything seemed just so ridiculous at the moment. I was lying in a bed of seaweed, in a cave on an alien planet, with a seaman I had *fucked* and enjoyed, and I had to explain to him what I meant by *kick your ass.*

But I didn't get a chance. As my giggles subsided, I was distracted by the look in Sahcor's eyes. "Please stop looking at me as though I'm dying," I said and rolled my head to the side to watch him. "I'm okay."

"I'm—"

I held up a finger. "If you say *I'm sorry* one more time..."

His lip twitched. "Yes, I know, you'll kick my ass."

"Right." I laughed.

"How can I make it up to you?"

I tapped my chin. "Gee, Sahcor, I don't know. I mean, rescuing me more than once, feeding me, welcoming me into your home, treating my wounds, and giving me the best orgasms of my life might not be enough."

A snarl escaped his throat, his sharp teeth exposed as the corner of his lip lifted. "You wish for more orgasms."

"That's not what I... *Sahcor!*" I squealed as he leaped on the bed, lifted me by the hips, and gently draped my legs over his shoulders, being additionally careful with my wounded leg. His breath was hot against my pussy, and I moaned, trembling as he took a deep, shuddering intake of air before he sighed. I groaned and tilted my head back as the scent of his pheromones wafted between us and filled the space around me. I breathed deep and let them into my lungs, wanting them to consume me like my thoughts and feelings of Sahcor had.

"Sahcor, you don't have to…" My sentence ended in a moan as he languidly licked up my pussy, my hips jumping against his face as he hit my clit.

"I *want* to, Misha. I want to taste your cunt, and I want my tongue covered in your cum."

There was no chance to respond, and I grabbed fistfuls of his hair as he plunged his tongue into me, swirling and thrusting it like a man starving. "God… *fuck…*" Shamelessly, I ground my pussy against his face, seeking everything he had to give. Every time I pushed against him, the rumbling growl in his chest would get louder, and his hands tightened where he held me as he moved up to lick, nip, and suck at my clit. It was sensation overload, Sahcor taking what he wanted while giving me *everything.*

I came. *Hard.* And as promised, he pushed his tongue inside me as I did, licking up every trace of my cum as he hummed, and the vibrations added another level of sensation.

But he didn't stop and started again with another few lazy licks, my hips bucking against his face every time he hit my clit.

"Sahcor…"

"Shh, my mate. Let me pleasure you while you rest."

There were downsides to this alien planet.

But I'll be damned if I could think of any of them right now.

CHAPTER 19

SAHCOR

Misha was more than I could have dreamed possible.

Years of being alone, keeping myself moving one day at a time by focusing on the needs of those species displaced from their homes, motivated by the desire to make sure the Ghaal didn't get their hands on any more innocent beings, and I was rewarded.

I wasn't a superstitious being and didn't gather things in multiples of six by some custom, the origins of which were long-forgotten. By Ghaal standards, I should have no luck, well-being, and nothing to guide me toward a brighter day.

Yet here she lay, a female, *my* female, in my bed—one of her slender arms thrown over her forehead as she slept, her entire body relaxed after yesterday, when I kept her in bed and licked her sweet cunt whenever she got restless. Her leg needed to heal, an injury she wouldn't have had I thought things through more thoroughly. My brows furrowed as I watched her roll over in her sleep and tuck herself into a ball. I never used to act hastily and always took my time to think over every situation.

Taking Misha into the ocean at night had been a mistake, then when she almost drowned, I was panicking to the point of not being able to think straight.

My mate had taken over my mind, muddled me, made me possessive, and reduced me to animal when it came to her pleasure and safety.

And I couldn't find it within myself to care about changing that.

Because I would be whatever she needed me to be.

The sun had risen, warming the waters and bringing out the most delicious fish, and I had gathered a small feast for Misha. Moving to the side of the bed, I peeled away the dried weeds from her leg and sighed with satisfaction as I saw the wound had almost healed over but not gone. Misha didn't seem to heal as quickly as I did, but a stronger covering than a scab was evident.

Smiling, I replaced the covering. Today, I was taking Misha out of the cave to show her some of the continent. I couldn't imagine she would take well to being told she had to rest another full day. So, we would do some exploring together, then we would come back and bathe, and perhaps she would let me bend her over the bank of the stream again and fuck her.

My cock twitched as the vivid thought passed through my mind, the memories of her slick wetness surrounding and squeezing me.

Misha groaned, rolled over again, blinked away sleep, and smiled when she saw me.

"Good morning," she whispered.

"Hello, my mate. I have gathered you breakfast."

Misha pushed herself onto an elbow and looked around me. "That's a lot of food, Sahcor. How many people are we feeding?"

"Just us. You'll need your strength."

"Why? Oh!" Misha sat upright and clapped her hands together. "Are we going out to do something?"

"I'm going to take you to see some parts of the continent." Misha's face went through a series of changes as she struggled with emotions I couldn't name. My heart sank. I thought she would be excited, but her smile had quickly faded into concern, and her teeth bit against her bottom lip. "Did I do something wrong?"

Misha's eyes cleared as she looked at me and rested her hand on my forearm. "No, no, of course not. Sorry. I'm excited, I really am," she reassured me when I couldn't bring myself to smile. "But I just had this pang of fear..." Misha lifted her other hand to her chest, and her lip twisted as though in pain. "Leaving the cave and getting closer to the Ghaal..."

"I'm not taking you anywhere near the Ghaal," I snarled out the words, and her eyes were wide when she looked at my face. Taking a deep breath, I cupped her cheek in my palm, and a growl rumbled through my chest when she leaned into the touch. "We're going to where we bathed, but farther. We are a long way from the colony, and I won't let you from my sight. I wish for you to see my home."

The way she looked up at me stole my breath and constricted my throat.

Trust. Happiness.

Desire.

I couldn't help as the growl grew louder. "Do not look at me like that, my mate, or we may never leave this cave."

She chuckled, her eyes brighter now I had reassured her she wouldn't be in danger. "I thought you would've wanted a break after yesterday." Her smile changed into a pout. "You didn't even let me return the favor and put my mouth on *you*."

My breath was stolen from my lungs. I leaned forward, curled my fingers into her hair, and inhaled deeply as I bumped my nose against her neck. "I would lick your cunt for the rest of my days if you let me."

Misha gasped, and the sweet scent of her arousal hit my nostrils. "God…" Her small tongue darted out and wet her lips. "You get grumpy because I *look* at you funny, yet you can say things like *that*."

I said nothing but ran my tongue along her collarbone and up her throat. "Eat breakfast, Misha, before I devour you."

She hesitated, and I almost laughed. Catching my expression, Misha laughed and shoved a hand into my chest. I shifted out of the way so she could climb out of bed. She stood in front of me, testing the weight on her leg before she straightened. She was gloriously naked, and the purple lights cast colors across her skin and made her look like *me*. A possessive growl rumbled through my chest. Her nipples tightened as I watched her, and while her fingers curled in toward her palms, she didn't attempt to cover herself from me.

"I don't have any clothes yet," Misha said, her neck craning when I stood and closed the space between us. "I can't go exploring naked."

I'm sure she knew what I was thinking without me needing to say anything, so I simply grinned at her. "I made you some clothes."

"Oh..." Her smile was shy. "Thank you."

I held up what I'd been working on, and as Misha reached out for it, her face dropped. "What..." she swallowed, and when she looked back at me, her smile was forced, but there was a cheeky glint in her eye. "Are you serious?"

Certain I was missing something, my mind traveled through the conversations we'd had. Unable to find what Misha found so amusing, I said nothing and waited patiently as she pulled the clothes on. It was a simple loin-covering design to cover her pussy and ass from being scratched, and cut up at the thighs to allow for maximum freedom of movement. I'd made her some boots out of the same material to protect her soft feet.

I didn't see the issue.

Misha laughed as she pulled on the loin covering, and my lips twitched as I tried to meet her smile, still trying to figure out what I'd done wrong. She didn't appear angry, but her amusement at the clothes had me second-guessing.

Misha held her arms out to her sides and jiggled her breasts at me. She laughed harder when my jaw dropped as my eyes followed the hypnotizing motion of her breasts. "Aren't you forgetting something?"

"Misha..." My confusion seemed to amuse her further, and she pulled the boots on as she danced over to me before she planted her palms against my chest.

"I'm not laughing at you, Sahcor." She chuckled, and I frowned. It certainly seemed like she was. "I think I can safely assume your choice of design was born from what you know and not because you want to have an eyeful of my tits all day."

"I could not replicate your clothes with the materials I had. I'd need furs, but I don't keep them here."

"Oh, oh no, you sweet man." Misha grabbed my cheeks and pushed them together so my lips pouted before she kissed me. "I'm not angry or upset. I'm sorry I laughed, but it just reminded me of *Tarzan* or something."

"I don't understand." As my expression contorted, Misha laughed again. There were times I could forget Misha was an alien being from another planet. The times I had my face buried between her legs or when we ate or played together, but sometimes she behaved so strangely. The reminder she wasn't of this planet slammed back into my consciousness, and with it, the awareness she was abducted from her home.

When a wave of irrational anger washed over me, I shook my head to rid myself of it.

My mate was confusing to me, but she was smiling and happy, and once she let go of my face, she ran her hands down over her new clothes. "It's like a flexible miniskirt," she muttered and chuckled to herself again. "Okay, I'll make you a deal."

I held her eye contact, hoping for an explanation about the confusing interaction from moments before. Misha smiled and rubbed her thumb over my cheek again. "Relax, Sahcor, everything is fine."

"I am confused."

"I promise I'll tell you all about Tarzan, but first, I have a favor to ask."

"Anything."

"When we get back tonight, I need you to weave me a covering for my boobs, okay? A girl needs support." Reaching forward, I cupped her breasts in my hands, relishing in the gasp she released before she gave me a teasing smile. "We can't walk about all day with you holding my boobs."

My lips curved into a smile. "Would it be so bad?"

She released another laugh. The joyful sound danced across the air between us, and I relaxed. Misha was happy. She was *happy* with *me*.

Misha patted my chest again. "Come on, big guy, let's eat some breakfast."

CHAPTER 20

MISHA

Folding one arm over my chest, I held Sahcor's hand with the other as he wound his way through the narrow cave system. Blinking in the sunlight as we emerged, I took a grateful breath of the ocean air, closed my eyes for a moment, and tilted my face toward the sun.

Sahcor had taken excellent care of me yesterday in more ways than one, but I needed to be outdoors, as eventually being stuck in a cave would drive me crazy. I smiled as I took Sahcor's hand, and he led me toward the stream where we had bathed the other day—maybe he knew if he tried to keep me indoors one more day, he'd have a fight on his hands.

Although any physical altercation between us wouldn't get far, Sahcor would have me pinned to the ground in seconds.

A shudder ran up my spine, and I pressed my legs together.

I wouldn't mind that at all.

There was no bridge or means to cross the stream short of walking through it, so I followed Sahcor's lead, trying not to slip on the bank on the way down. "Can we bathe on the way back?" I asked, and Sahcor nodded as he helped me onto the opposite side of the stream.

"Of course."

Immediately, my mind was flooded with images of Sahcor bending me over the bank and taking me again, the delicious stretch of him inside me, and the feel of warmth as his cum flooded my pussy.

Fuck.

Inhaling, I caught his scent in the air. Why did he have to smell so damn good? It was distracting.

The grasses soon gave way to thin, pale trees. The bark looked like it would have a feathered texture, and they fanned at the top like a paintbrush. Small creatures flitted in and out of the foliage, but despite the openness of the trees, I couldn't see them properly. Their chirping made me smile as I thought of the birdlife that lived on my farm. Little things reminded me of home, and while a stab of sadness still twisted in my gut, it was also nice to have these familiar things.

It made this place feel more like home.

We walked leisurely, simply taking in the surroundings and enjoying each other's company. I asked about a few species of plants that looked interesting and wondered out loud why I hadn't seen more wildlife.

"Because of me," Sahcor said, the words ending with a snarl.

"What do you mean?"

"Part of keeping species away from the colony means scaring away *all* species. There aren't many natives left, but any predators or animals with a level of intelligence won't stay around here. I warn them away, if not with words and language, then by acting like a predator to them."

His face twisted, and my heart ached. "You hate it."

"I don't like scaring innocent beings."

I squeezed his hand instead of some words of comfort that probably wouldn't work anyway. Sahcor squeezed gently back, and again, we fell into an easy silence.

The morning drew on slowly, and the lashings of the waves against the shore became a permanent backdrop to our walk. The mainland was coming into clearer view every minute, and with it, an anxiety that each step only seemed to exacerbate. It felt safe here. Although Sahcor's cave was technically attached to the mainland, sometimes it felt like an island. But seeing the peninsula stretch out in front and behind me—a road directly to me, if the Ghaal should think to take it—brought on panic.

I often covered my anxieties with humor—a tool I had used on the Moek ship when the other girls were falling into pits of depression, and I could see the pain on their faces. If I could make them laugh or smile for even a moment, they would hurt less. But eventually, even that didn't help, and when my anxiety took over, I couldn't find the energy for it.

But here, on this strange planet with Sahcor, with the ocean air whipping the loose strands of hair around my face, my funny little reed skirt and breasts exposed, and all our food coming directly from nature, I thought I should try something to combat my anxiety I had rarely done on Earth.

Talk about it.

"Sahcor," I whispered, hating how my voice was already beginning to waiver, as if the sheer act of opening my mouth to speak would unleash a tidal wave of emotion I couldn't contain. "Can I be honest with you?"

Either Sahcor already knew me better than I thought, or I was a terrible actor. He stopped abruptly, turned to face me, and immediately kneeled so we were face to face. "Of course."

"I'm frightened."

His expression twisted again. "I'll protect you."

"No. I mean, yes, I know you will. *Shit.*" I swiped some hair from my face, and my gaze automatically flickered to the distance beyond the beach, where I knew the Ghaal colony was. "Every turn I seem to take on this planet, I'm getting taken or attacked by something. I don't want to spend my entire life in a cave, but I can't shake the feeling that I'm in danger."

Sahcor said nothing. Once again, a thousand silent thoughts seemed to pass through his mind as he analyzed the situation and *me.*

I caught the thoughts before he said them. "But that's just it, isn't it? I *am* in danger here, and I may *always* be in danger here."

"I'll protect you." This time his words were delivered with force and an aggression I don't think I'd heard from him before.

"I know you will. I just... I need to take small steps, you know? A little bit at a time. I don't think I'm ready for the mainland yet. Maybe tomorrow? Maybe just the beach?"

"Do you wish to go back to the cave now?"

I released the breath caught in my chest, making it ache. What did I expect? For Sahcor to judge me and my worries? For him to tell me I was weak and pathetic and should be stronger? He wouldn't do any of those things. Just because my stupid, anxious brain was telling me that, it didn't mean it's what *he* thought of me.

I knew what I wanted to do with the rest of the day, but again, I wrestled with the idea that if I wasn't *achieving* anything, I was doing something inherently wrong. It was nearly impossible to switch from the hustle and bustle of everyday life to absolute silence and solidarity without the mind at least attempting a rebellion.

Sahcor was watching me, not pushing me for an answer or looking impatient in the slightest. He also had duties, but did he still, really? Because if there *were* humans here before us, and if the Ghaal knew we were compatible, they surely wouldn't keep engaging the Moeks to abduct species. They would spend their time here, trying to capture the girls and me again.

Swallowing, I wished a silent prayer to God knows who that the girls were safe and mentally reassured myself I was doing the right thing by keeping my distance.

What did I want to do for the rest of the day?

My lips curved into a smile as I looked at Sahcor. "How about another lazy day in the stream, talking and eating and—"

The snarl he released was animal, and my nipples tightened at the intensity of his gaze. "And fucking."

"Well, yes." I looked around guiltily as if there would be someone here to tell me I was being selfish. But there was no one, only us.

Sahcor was on his feet and tugged me back the way we had come with a hastier gait than he had left the cave with.

We didn't bother to enter the stream under the pretense of bathing this time. Sahcor and I would certainly bathe, but only after I'd had my fill of incredible orgasms and his amazing alien cock.

Which is a sentence I never thought would cross my mind.

"Fuck, Sahcor. Harder." I panted, and my fingers gripped into his forearms.

On my back on the bank of the stream, once again, the mud was increasing around me as the water splashed over the soil, and my laugh at the feeling of it morphed into a squeal after a particularly harsh thrust from Sahcor. He'd learned if he entered me fully and ground his hips against mine from this position, the bumps on his cock would rub against my clit. I swear my eyes rolled back into my head as he did this, and the fullness of having him stretch made me moan as my leg twitched under the assault to my clit.

Sahcor's brow was furrowed almost permanently as he watched where his cock sank into my pussy. His large hands were wrapped around my waist as he pinned me down and kept me still, forcing my body to respond.

"Going to make you rounded with my child, my mate," he muttered, the possessive growl running through his chest louder than ever.

"Fuck..." I stared at him, my eyes wide. Those words shouldn't turn me on as much as they did, but *fuck me,* I was practically dripping around him. He pulled out a bit only to slam into me a few times before he returned to grinding those delicious bumps against my clit. "I'm gonna... I'm gonna come..." I whispered before I gasped as he pulled my trembling leg over his shoulder, tilted forward, and increased the pressure on my clit. I cried out as my pleasure peaked, and the orgasm sent me into a twitching, moaning mess as my pussy clamped around Sahcor's cock.

He thrust in harder, hitting all the right spots inside me as my cries reached a new pitch. I think he tried to talk, but instead, only a guttural moan was released, and with another hard thrust, he came, and the rush of his warm cum pulsed inside me. Sahcor pushed deeper, and I cried out, clinging onto his arms as he held me on him, keeping his cum inside me.

Slumping back onto the bank, I brushed my fingertips over where his hands still held me. Sahcor went to withdraw, and I gripped his wrists, tilting my head to look at him. "No," I whispered, wrapped my legs around him, and pressed my heels into his ass, "Keep it inside."

Sahcor relaxed with a smile on his face I hadn't seen before. As he closed his eyes, I did, too, and laid back to relish in the stretch of him and the warmth of his thick cum inside me. His skin was smooth under my hands, and I kept brushing my fingers over the back of his hands, humming my contentment.

It was probably beyond a bad idea to want this, given all the dangers.

But once the idea of a child with Sahcor had planted itself in my mind, I really wanted it to be true.

CHAPTER 21

MISHA

Stretching my arms above my head the following morning, I intentionally moved so my breasts slightly swayed as Sahcor tried to tie the top he'd fashioned around my chest. He growled, I laughed, and his eyes darted to mine as if he knew exactly what I was doing. With a swift motion, he leaned forward and swiped his tongue across my nipple, making me jump.

He finished the tie, and I dropped my arms and looked down at the top. It was like a boob tube made of reeds, and my stomach was still exposed above my equally as wild-looking skirt. I laughed. "I feel like I'm going to a jungle-themed nightclub or something."

Confusion crossed Sahcor's face, and this wasn't helped when I pumped my arms above my head, chanting *oonce, oonce, oonce, oonce* like the bass of a generic dance song. Cupping his face in my hands, I kissed his soft lips. "You're so damn cute when you're confused."

"You do so many strange things," he murmured.

"Yes, but you still love me," I said with a flourish of my hand and brush over his chest before I froze on the spot, realizing too late what I'd said. Did those words have the same meaning here? Would Sahcor understand the significance of them?

"Yes," he said simply, a look of intensity in his eyes as I slowly turned to face him fully.

"Me too," I whispered. It was all I could manage at that moment, and from the growl that started in his chest again and his lip lifting into a snarl, I'd say it was enough. I swallowed, eager to get past this. Of course, I had feelings for Sahcor. I was facing a lifetime here with him and the prospect of a family, and rather than upsetting me, the idea excited me. Subconsciously, I placed a hand on my stomach, and Sahcor's hands twitched as he followed the movement as if he wanted to touch me there too. He seemed to be able to tell if I was pregnant or not through touch, judging by the look of disappointment he'd had last time he'd touched me like that.

Before he could move, I dropped my hand and smiled up at him. "Shall we go?"

Sahcor took another silent moment to continue staring at me, those moments when an entire world of things would pass unsaid across his eyes. But somehow, he didn't need to talk, and I could read him. He returned my smile, a small and gentle look, before he held out his hand to take mine and again led me through the maze that exited the cave. We'd woken early this morning, and the cave walls were cool after the night air had been on them, and every brush of my bare arms sent a shiver through me. The sun was only just coming up as we emerged onto the peninsula, a haze of orange in the distance which cast the ocean in an impossibly dark shadow.

"Are you okay?" Sahcor asked. I nodded and squeezed his hand as we started to walk.

My anxiety yesterday had left me embarrassed, and no matter how much my stomach churned and my chest ached with every steadying breath, I was determined to step foot onto shore today. We'd stay on the beach, but I needed to prove to myself I could do this. The longer I took babying myself, the more I would build things up in my mind and the harder it would be. I didn't want to spend my entire life on this strip of land and in a cave.

The only way to get past this was to push myself.

But my comfort zone is so comfy.

We walked slowly and leisurely, but I still couldn't help the sharp intake of breath when we passed the place we'd been yesterday. I said nothing. Sahcor also remained silent and responded only with another squeeze of my hand. I didn't need him to tell me what I already knew.

I'll protect you. We can turn back at any point.

When the beach came into clearer focus, my steps faltered before I came to a stop. "Can we uh…" I twisted my fingers together and glanced down at my body, but even my weaved nightclub attire couldn't distract me from the nerves. "Stop for a moment… just have a drink of water?"

Sahcor nodded and pulled me closer to him before we sat on the spot, the area only partially shaded by the thin, brushy trees, before he handed me the water bag. I took a grateful drink, handed it back, and leaned back on my palms so I could stare at the beach. "They don't know where you live, right?"

"No."

I nodded, still looking at the beach.

"We can turn back, Misha." Sahcor brushed his fingers up my arm, waiting for me to make eye contact before he continued, "You've come so much farther than yesterday… there's no shame in turning back."

My brows drew together. *Can he read me that easily?*

I was comforted by the idea Sahcor could see past me into the parts I hid but also nervous at reaching a level of intimacy in such a short time— something I never thought possible.

"No." I slapped my palms on my knees as I stood and offered Sahcor a tight smile. "I want to do this."

It was easier to relax once we were moving. Sitting still and staring at the beach like it represented imminent danger and everything nasty on this continent wasn't helping.

"I have something to show you," Sahcor said as we reached the rocky outcrop that descended onto the beach.

"Yeah?" Not as nimble as the Synth, I couldn't talk much as we moved over the rocks and needed to use all my concentration not to slip or face plant.

"The creatures printed on your old clothes... tell me about them."

"Oh," I gasped out, my heart lifting immediately. "Horses! Didn't I tell you about them already?"

"A little, but tell me more."

"Horses have been a huge part of human culture for thousands of years. They're pets and companions, but so much more than that. They're useful for agriculture and transportation, right up to racing and sporting events. They're just so beautiful and fascinating. Did I tell you I had a riding school where children would come and learn to ride horses?"

"For what purpose?"

I chuckled. He sounded so formal. "For fun and because they love horses." I sighed as I lowered myself over another rock. "Then there was Charlie, my baby boy... he's fifteen now."

Sahcor recoiled. "Horses are still infants at fifteen years?"

"No, no." I had to stop climbing down to give myself a moment to laugh, my fingers clutching my side. "*Baby...* as in an endearing term. He was my baby when he was a baby, and he's my baby no matter how old he is."

"I understand," Sahcor said, even though his expression betrayed him.

He didn't.

Thinking of Charlie was bringing on sadness I didn't want to feel, and before I choked up, I needed to redirect the conversation. "Why do you ask?"

"There's a creature here, the oarka, that the images on your clothes reminded me of. One of the few native species that remained after the wars and a distant relative to the oarke who live further inland."

I couldn't help but gasp. "Have you domesticated them?"

Sahcor gave me an odd look. "No. They are wild animals."

"Don't you have pets here?"

"The Ghaal had no need for pets. Animals are a

food source only."

I hummed. "It's so strange to me that a civilization can be so advanced yet still be missing some of the fundamentals humans have. Pets are important companionship. I can't imagine being in my home and not having a pet."

"There are no pets in my cave."

"There's you, and that's close enough." I laughed as his brow furrowed further. "I'm kidding. You're so cute."

One more drop and my boots hit the sand, damp and heavy with the water that rushed around the rocks' base. Following Sahcor further onto the beach, I hesitated as we reached the part where the rocks thinned, and we were about to step onto the open sand. I felt exposed and vulnerable, and I bit my lip against the rising anxiety.

"I will protect you," Sahcor said again, and I forced my shoulders to relax. I smiled and took his hand before stepping out into the sunlight with him.

"I need a distraction," I said, looking up at him. "Show me the horses."

We had to move farther along the beach than I had initially planned to locate the oarka, and with every step along the soft sand, I could feel my nervousness growing. But Sahcor gripped my hand even as his gaze remained determinedly fixed at the distance. I reminded myself he could see much farther than I could, and even at the slightest hint of danger, we simply had to move into the ocean, and Sahcor could whisk me away to safety.

I relaxed slightly.

"Are they friendly?" I whispered, unsure if my voice would be enough to startle the oarka. I knew it was crazy to expect the oarka to look like horses, but Sahcor had said the print on my pajamas reminded him of them. Tilting my head, I watched three of them move along the edge of the beach, plucking dry grass from between the rocks of the cliff face. They were sandy in color like the sand on Earth, not the grayish tinge of sand here. But thinking of the wispy trees around the stream we bathed in, I could see how they could disappear between them. At first glance, the oarka were more like large dogs than anything, with shaggy, light-colored, thick fur that covered their muscular hides.

Was it the fluff of white hair on top of their heads that ran down the back of their necks that made Sahcor think of horses? And they did appear to have hooves.

"They're not aggressive," Sahcor said, although I frowned since that wasn't much of an answer. "You can get quite near them, and they won't flee or attack unless they feel threatened."

"Do you use them for food?"

He shook his head. "Too much meat for me, and I prefer to eat fresh meat."

Straightening my shoulders, I let go of Sahcor's hand and approached the oarka. Two of the three lifted their heads to watch me approach but otherwise made no movement beyond their jaws' slow, steady motions as their teeth worked against the grasses. I stopped only to pick a handful of grass and moved toward them, holding it out in front of me.

"Hi, babies," I said, unable to help the *coo* in my voice which always happened when I was near an animal. "Are you gonna let me get close to you?"

Earning animals' trust was a game of patience. I'd have to find something they liked to eat, something better than grass they couldn't acquire, and come to the same spot every day and offer it to them. Eventually, they would let me touch them.

Maybe I could even ride one.

I felt a surge of happiness at the idea that clashed inside me with the absurdity of the thought. It wasn't *impossible* and existed well within the realms of possibility. But the image of myself riding half naked across a beach on top of a shaggy, hoofed dog was too much, and I bit back the giggle that threatened to surface, keeping my lips sealed in case showing teeth was a sign of aggression.

One of the oarka snorted and stomped its foot, and I stopped, remaining still and holding the grass out. The handful I'd picked included a smattering of small white flowers that weren't on the ones they were eating, and they seemed to get its interest. Its large nostrils twitched as it sniffed in my direction.

"Come on…" I cooed, shaking the grass slightly. "Come and get a snack."

All three were watching me now, and when the one closest took a hesitant step toward me, I froze, barely daring to breathe. With a strange whinny that sounded almost like a chainsaw revving up, it lurched forward and clamped its teeth over the grass before it jerked its head away and trotted a few paces behind the other two.

It stared at me as it chewed, and I smiled. "Good girl… I think. That's enough for now. I'll see if I can find some treats for you."

Unable to wipe the smile from my face, I backed away a few steps before I turned my back on the oarkas and returned to Sahcor. He watched me with the most curious expression, but he relaxed and smiled when I approached him and held his hand out for me to take.

"Do they eat anything else? A treat we can bring them?"

Sahcor glanced at the oarka, and I followed his gaze. They had returned to grazing, having neither fled nor followed me after I left. "I'm not sure, but maybe they'd like the gladvin berries."

"Can we come back tomorrow and grab some on the way?"

"Of course. Do you wish to go home?"

"No," I said and turned to rest my back against Sahcor's chest as I watched the oarka eat. "I think we can stay out for a while. Maybe we can find more flowers for them or something."

Sahcor was smiling when I tilted my head to look up at him. "You are so strange, my mate."

"Says the ocean man with gills," I teased.

A rumble ran through his chest as he chuckled, wrapped his arms around me, and held me against him.

CHAPTER 22

MISHA

We spent the afternoon scouring the cliff face for the grasses the oarka were eating, looking specifically for the ones with abundant small flowers. Every time I returned to the small herd, I was greeted with the same trepidation at the start. But slowly, they started looking up as I approached, the nervous movement of their hooves against the sand becoming less frequent.

I felt safe with Sahcor so close.

So, I moved farther down the beach.

We were still well away from the Ghaal colony, and while I couldn't help the occasional nervous glances up the beach or the jerking of my head whenever I heard an unfamiliar sound, the day moved along at a calm and steady pace. Sahcor and I sat and ate together after he dived into the water to get some fish. I hugged my arms around myself, trying to shrink against the rocks and disappear until he emerged from the water.

I couldn't help laughing as he approached, a fish between his teeth and another in each hand.

He removed the fish from his mouth. "Why are you laughing?"

"Because you looked silly with the fish in your mouth." I giggled again and pressed the back of my hand against my mouth as he watched me for a moment. There was enough of a twitch of his lip that indicated a slight smile, and I laughed openly.

As he cleaned the fish, I looked at the small pile of grasses next to me. "Can we eat these flowers too?"

Sahcor scrunched up his nose. "You can, but it won't be easy."

"What do you mean?" I lifted the stalk toward my nose and sniffed at the flower. It looked innocent enough, but when I glanced at Sahcor, there was a twinkle in his eyes.

"Why don't you try it?" he said.

My eyes narrowed. "I feel like I'm being set up." I sniffed the plant again. *What the hell, right?* I'm always up for a joke. I popped a single flower into my mouth and rolled it around on my tongue.

My eyebrow arched as I waited for the joke.

It tasted like nothing.

And then...

"Oh my *God!*" Frantically, I stuck my tongue out and started swiping at it, trying to empty my mouth of the plant which had expanded after it hit the moisture in my mouth and felt like cotton wool. It stuck to my tongue and cheeks, and by the time I rid my mouth of it, I was gagging. "Oh my God, *Sahcor,* I will *get you for this."* Rolling to my side, I reached out and snatched the water bag from him, rinsing and spitting until my mouth was clear.

Sahcor was laughing openly, and I couldn't help but laugh too. "I'm going to kick your ass," I muttered, running my tongue along the roof of my mouth and smacking against the remaining dryness. "This fish better be good."

In response, Sahcor simply kept laughing and handed me some. I frowned at him before taking it as the pile of edible meat seemed impossibly small compared to the size of the fish.

"Hacku," he said, waving the fish in front of me. "My favorite. The best there is."

Taking the meat, I placed it on my tongue and groaned as it practically melted, the delicate flavor *almost* like fish from home, but sweet too. Sahcor nodded and smiled at my reaction before offering me more. "They are hard to catch and have large internal organs, so not much flesh but are an excellent treat."

"Damn right, they are." I ate more, then refused the next portion he offered, staring Sahcor down until he ate some himself.

"Would you like some more?"

I did want more. I really did, but I also didn't want Sahcor to make unnecessary efforts when there were fish around that were easier to catch and tasty enough. Sahcor stood when he saw my indecision. "I'll get a few more for my mate."

He returned my smile, and I tucked myself back against the rocks as he bolted toward the ocean again.

The crashing of the waves was relaxing, and I settled against the warmth of the rocks, adjusting until I found a nook that curved against my back.

"Hello?"

Startled, I sat bolt upright and scraped my shoulder against the rock in the process. I ignored the sting and curled my hands into the sand next to my thighs.

I could have *sworn* I heard a voice.

A *human* voice.

Had the other girls found me?

A quick glance in the direction of the Ghaal colony was enough to have my stomach in knots. Did I answer the voice or try to hide? Do I let the girls find me and then tell them to leave me alone or simply run so they never see me? Indecision crippled me and held me still. My eyes darted toward the ocean. Where was Sahcor? I needed him to help me decide.

"Hello? Is anyone there? *Please.*"

This time, the voice was edged with desperation, and I bit my lip.

What if they are hurt?

I couldn't tell who it was. I'd heard the other girls' voices for only seconds when we were in the hallway of the alien ship before we were pushed into the release pods. Maybe it was Erica?

"Oh please, please let someone be there. I don't know how much farther I can go on..."

There was a distinct sob after that, and my heart clenched. *"Fuck,"* I whispered. Shuffling out from the rocks, I stood and looked about.

"Hello?" I called back. "Where are you?"

"Oh, *thank you*," the female voice hitched with relief before another sob. "I'm snagged in some bushes. Please. I dragged myself this far. I'm hurt."

"Fuck," I muttered again and threw another glance at the ocean before I followed the cliff face to where the grasses and harsh bushes grew in packs. "Where are you?"

"Here, here. I can hear you. You're so close."

"If you just hold on, my friend can help us." I indicated the ocean, even though since I couldn't see who was speaking, I doubted she could see me.

"Please don't *leave me.* I'm hurt. *Please* just help get me out of here."

My body shifted around as I turned back and forth between the ocean and the bushes. Anxiety was bubbling in my stomach and mixed uncomfortably with the fish and a large dose of guilt. I'd try to do the right thing by distancing myself from the girls, and I couldn't leave one stranded and injured. I twisted my hands together and gnawed on my bottom lip. "I really should call my friend..."

"*Please help...*"

"Sahcor!" I cried out his name, but there was no response, and I couldn't see his head above the water. *Why did I let him hunt for something that was so far out?*

"Can you wait?" I asked into the bushes, bending down and trying to see between the twisted foliage. "Are you bleeding?"

"I can't feel my legs. There's a lot of blood."

"*Shit,*" I muttered, twisting my fingers together. Her voice was getting weaker, and if she *dragged* herself here, how long had she been hurt? My seconds and minutes of indecision could be the difference between life and death. And waiting for Sahcor to come back? If she were dead when I found her, I'd never forgive myself.

"Dammit." I grabbed two handfuls of the bushes and tried to ignore the sting of the sharp, thin branches against my palm. "Where—" I screamed as my wrists were grabbed, and I was dragged into the dense center of the bushes.

A palm was slapped over my mouth, and my stomach churned at the scent that overpowered that of the ocean, like rotten cherries soaked in alcohol.

Ghaal.

Screaming against the palm, I writhed and struggled, and my legs scratched up as I scrambled against the bushes.

"Stay still." A male voice from behind me spoke directly into my ear as an arm wrapped around my chest. "Or we'll kill the Synth." I stilled, and the Ghaal chuckled as I whined against his hand. "Good work, Kupa." He threw the words over his shoulder, and a female chuckled.

"Thank you, master," she uttered, then said something in her language.

The third Ghaal came into my vision and crouched next to me as he shuffled forward. He removed something from his pocket and held it in front of him. There was a buzz, and the air shimmered, but nothing else happened. "The Synth won't see anything if he looks in here now," he said.

The Ghaal behind me tugged me backward, farther into the bush, the twigs scratching my arms and legs. "Good to see you again, human," he said, the sneer evident in his voice even though I couldn't see his face. "Kupa, here, was more than willing to help. She's infertile but doesn't want to see our species die off either."

"I'd also rather not see you fuck this disgusting creature, master," she whispered.

The male Ghaal snarled at her, then hissed for her to be quiet as Sahcor could be heard calling for me.

"Misha?" Something dropped on the sand as the pounding of his feet grew louder. "*Misha?*"

I started crying at the panic in his voice, but when I tried to call out, the Ghaal pressed harder against my mouth and crushed me against his chest until it was a struggle to breathe.

Sahcor was snarling and growling, and the bushes in front of us vibrated as he fought against those farther to the front. The Ghaal used the sound of Sahcor's panicked attempts to break through the bushes to cover us as they moved farther backward. The second male still held the tool in front of us and kept the air shimmering, apparently hiding our location from Sahcor.

"*Misha!*" Sahcor's snarl was broken momentarily by an anguished sob that tore at my heart before the growling started again, louder and more insistent than I'd heard it before. With an inhuman roar, his feet started pounding against the sand, and he ran off toward the Ghaal colony.

I tried to hold in my sigh. Sahcor assumed I had

been taken and was immediately on the way to rescue me.

I had to stay calm.

Sahcor would come for me.

CHAPTER 23

SAHCOR

The Ghaal colony.

It was the only thought on my mind, and I alternated between running along the beach and diving into the ocean to cover more ground faster. Misha had disappeared, and I'd searched and called, but their scent gave them away. The rancid smell of their skin lingered in the area, along with the metallic bite of blood. The Ghaal was there, Misha was missing, and there was no way it was a coincidence.

Rage ate away at my insides, bubbling together with self-hatred. I'd been complacent about going back into the ocean a second time for more fish. Misha seemed happy and relaxed, and I wanted to please her.

But I was a terrible mate.

Once she was safe again, perhaps it would be better to take her to her friends and maybe find Ilk or Lanir to look after her. I'm sure Misha would protest—the protective part of her would be steadfastly certain she needed to keep away from the other females to keep them safe. But she wasn't safe with me either, and certainly not this close to the colony.

My selfishness had again cost Misha her freedom.

And I would never forgive myself.

Misha was kind and forgiving and had stuck with me even when I blundered with her safety. I doubted everything about myself now. Every part of me I thought I knew fell apart the moment I saw her. I wasn't the thinker I thought I was and couldn't plan or take stock of a situation. Where was that Synth that had infiltrated the Ghaal colony more than once to learn? Where did he go? Because it couldn't have been me with the mistakes I kept making.

I had failed my mate.

But I wouldn't this time.

Unsure how the Ghaal was traveling, whether by foot or if they still had the remnants of some almost broken down transport system, I couldn't be sure if I arrived at the colony before they had even returned with Misha.

But they were expecting me.

A line of Ghaal waited as I exited the woodlands, and the area opened up to the colony. Emerging from between two buildings, I stepped into the remaining sunlight as it disappeared over the treetops toward the mountains and cast a large shadow over a portion of the colony.

"Where is she?" I snarled in my native tongue. Being here at night when I could move around almost undetected made me sick, but being here with the sun out made my skin crawl with awareness. These may have been the beings who created us, but they were also the beings who tortured us within an inch of our lives. The ones who drove us to violence we would have preferred not to engage in simply because we had to for us to escape with our lives.

Some of them had to die so we could live, and while I had never wanted to feel the thick roll of Ghaal blood on my hands again, right now, I would kill them all if it would save Misha.

But despite their dwindling technology, there was something they protected with as much fervor as their machines and equipment used to impregnate and experiment.

The toxin.

Delivered via a stab through our thick skin with a specially designed wand, the toxins were designed specifically for us Synths. They'd have no effect on the Ghaal, but once in our bloodstream, it would shut us down from the inside, attacking a fail-safe implanted in our DNA. With a full dose, we'd have minutes to live, and there was no cure.

Several Ghaal standing in a semicircle in an open part of the colony held these wands now, the near-invisible needle glinting off the remainder of the sunlight as they pointed them at me.

"Leave, Synth. We will not hesitate to kill you if you come any closer."

I growled. "You know I can't leave without her."

The small crowd parted as a Ghaal stepped forward. "I am Rah," he said and placed a hand on his chest. "Do you remember me?"

I stared at him. Of course, I didn't remember him. All the Ghaal who tortured us were faceless blobs because of the pain we endured. I didn't remember any of them in particular—they were all as violent as each other.

He bared his teeth in a horrifying simile of a

smile. "I have an offer for you." When I said nothing but simply curled my hands into fists, he continued, "You contain Ghaal DNA, the best of the best. It would be a shame to waste that. If you come with me, I'll allow you to breed the human female."

I roared a note of rage. "Let her *go.*"

Rah took another step forward, and despite my physical superiority, I found myself backing away from the monster in front of me. "It's what you want, isn't it? To fuck the female?"

I didn't want anything the Ghaal had to offer, and Misha wasn't *theirs* to offer to me like a prize or a piece of property to be borrowed. If she were going to birth my child, she would do it of her own free will, far away from the Ghaal.

"Let her go," I hissed out the words between clenched teeth.

Rah tilted his head at me, and the orange rings of color around his large pupils blazed as his anger seemed to intensify. The small weapon he held reflected the light as he rolled it around his fingers. My gaze was attracted to the movement—he wouldn't need to stab me deep or even anywhere near a vital organ for it to work.

Did the weapons still work?

Their technology was failing bit by bit, year by year.

If I assumed they were bluffing, and I was wrong, who would save Misha?

It was agony to take another step back from Rah, and he didn't continue to move forward. His eyes simply followed my movement as I took another step. Everything inside me was screaming to attack them, to unleash the violence I hadn't since my brothers and I escaped. But the risk was too great, and that risk was Misha. I would find another way, and while I suspected they wouldn't leave her unguarded again, I wouldn't give up.

"Keep your distance, Synth," Rah hissed out, brandishing the weapon between us. "You are no longer needed."

"I'll come for her. I'll come for her, and I won't stop."

Rah's eyes narrowed. "Then we will be forced to kill you."

The sound that escaped me was pure animal, reducing me to the primitive creature they treated us as. My nerves were on fire, and my skin crawled at their proximity until I was nothing more than a cornered animal. The internal battle between launching at them, trying to fight, or pulling back so I could devise a plan raged in my mind.

I scoffed. "You threaten me like taking my life would be a chore, when you and I both know you'd enjoy it."

Rah's grin widened. "You're right. I would gladly kill you all with great pleasure as revenge for the havoc you caused on our species."

"Don't blame us for your problems. You were killing yourselves off long before we were created."

Rah sneered as his smile faded. "It's a pity... you had such potential. Maybe we won't kill you... maybe we'll harvest you for the useful parts." He bared his teeth at me. "Maybe we'll make the human watch."

He released a laugh at my response, the force it was taking to hold myself back evident in how my muscles tensed.

"I'll come for her," I hissed out before I turned and disappeared into the woods.

As expected, there were sentries set to guard Misha in the lab this time. I internally chastised myself for falling for their trap last time, but while I was suspicious of their intentions with the lack of guards, I simply couldn't leave Misha there, and taking her was worth the risk.

My caution with my livelihood now had nothing to do with self-preservation and everything to do with simply knowing that Misha wouldn't be able to defend herself without me. I would lay down my life for her without a second thought, even though I knew she wouldn't forgive me for that, but I needed to stay alive, if only to save her.

I considered getting my brothers, but the time it would take could be deadly for Misha.

And I didn't know how much time I had.

Besides, this was my fight.

Dragging myself on my stomach through the undergrowth, I edged up to the lab where Misha had been kept last time, and I didn't doubt she was there now. Seven Ghaal were present around the building, and that was only what I could see. Around the corners there was undoubtedly more, their most precious cargo contained inside.

What were they doing to her in there?

Squashing down the snarl that rose in my chest took effort, and I winced as a slight sound escaped. The Ghaal closest paused in his step but didn't turn my way.

I needed a distraction.

"Get up, Synth."

My fingers curled into the soil as something was pushed into the back of my neck. Gritting my teeth, I took a moment to assess. The instrument was blunt, not a blade or a needle.

Not the weapon they needed.

My brother, Ilk, was steadfast against violence, and usually I would agree. But when broken down to my DNA and what I was created for, I was an animal made for breeding and treated as such initially.

And my mate was in trouble.

With a snarl, I rolled, reached up at the same time and clasped my hands around the Ghaal's head. His eyes widened in shock as I squeezed, and his hands came up to pathetically grip at mine. With a sharp jerk, I broke his neck and grabbed his body as it went limp before I gently lowered him to the ground and glanced around to see if I had been spotted.

The other Ghaal was looking and pointing in this direction.

Snarling, I looked around.

How had that Ghaal snuck up on me in the first place? I should have heard him coming.

Unless he was already here, waiting for me.

The area was coated in their scent, and if he were completely still, I wouldn't have known. My senses may be enhanced, but I wasn't invincible. I snarled as I remembered the moment Misha was taken. Was she right under my nose, and I could not see her? The Ghaal had cloaking devices once upon a time. Did they still work?

Several of the Ghaal now headed my way, their feet crunching over the undergrowth as they passed the boundary into the woodlands. Growling, I shoved the body of the Ghaal I had killed out of my way and ran.

I wouldn't give up, but a part of my mind was telling me the only way I could achieve this was with the help of my brothers. I shouldn't let my possessive nature take over my ability to think logically.

My mate is in trouble.

I didn't bother containing the roar as I moved through the woodlands.

I wanted the Ghaal to know I was near.

And that I was coming back.

MISHA

The sun had disappeared over the tree line by the time I was ushered into the prison in the Ghaal village. The walk had been mostly silent, and I bit my lip several times against the desire to scream and shout at the Ghaal. When we started moving at first, any time I would open my mouth, one of the male Ghaal would slap a hand over my face or simply shove me forward so any scream or sound I would make was interrupted as I hit the ground and grazed my knees and palms.

After the third time, I stood, brushed the sandy soil off my hands, and glared at the Ghaal.

"Something to say, human?" One of them sneered at me.

I responded by spitting at him and cried out when he retaliated by slapping me across the face. I fell again and stayed down for a moment, my breaths coming in rattling gasps as I tried to keep myself together.

Sahcor will come for me.

The Ghaal grabbed a handful of my hair, pulled, and forced me to my feet again. "Keep moving."

I did.

I had no real sense of the time, and my nerves remained on edge as my gaze darted around. Several Ghaal surrounded me, and any attempt to run would simply have me colliding with them.

"I need to use the bathroom," I announced after a while.

They didn't stop walking. "I don't care."

Dammit.

Curling my shoulder away from the Ghaal as they moved to shove me into the cell again, the same one I had been in last time, I glared at them as the large doors were closed with a heavy clang. A quick glance showed me the bars Sahcor had bent out of shape last time had been replaced. Not only that, but feet were moving around outside, no doubt the guards I didn't have before.

I guess they wouldn't be letting me escape so easily this time.

Sahcor will come for me.

It was the only thought that kept me sane, and I clutched onto it as I curled up in the corner of the cell, covered my eyes against the dim blue lighting from the circular lights on the walls with my palms, and brought my knees up to my chest.

Harsh words spoken in the Ghaal's unfamiliar language startled me awake. It was dark, but the blue light was enough to illuminate the cell as the doors creaked open. I scrambled to my feet, keeping my back pressed against the rear wall of the cell. My mind was still half asleep, and by the time I had registered the door had been opened, I should have considered bolting, but the door was already being closed again. Right before it closed, there was another burst of language, and a Ghaal was shoved into the cell with me.

He stumbled to his hands and knees and turned back to watch the door slam closed and lock with a click before he looked up at me.

Oh fuck no.

Panicking, I pressed myself harder against the wall, shook my head, and flattened my palms against the cold walls. There was nowhere for me to run, and wildly, my eyes shifted around the cell, desperate for anything I could use as a weapon.

Nothing.

"Don't fucking touch me," I cried out and pointed at him with a shaky finger.

The group of Ghaal was standing by the door, watching the exchange through the bars and laughing. I couldn't understand what they were saying, but from their tone and the gestures of their large hands, it sounded like they were egging him on.

The Ghaal on the floor pushed himself to his feet, stood at his full height, and stared at me with wide eyes. Something about him looked familiar, but the Ghaal all looked so similar, and what did it matter who he was anyway?

"Go on, Sol," one of the group said, making sure I could understand. "Fuck her hard."

My legs were shaking as I glanced back at Sol, finally placing him. They weren't all clones of each other—some taller, some shorter, different facial features, just like humans. But since I was their captive, I didn't bother to pay too much attention to them. But Sol, I remembered him. He was the one who had brought me a pillow last time I was here, the one who had spoken calmly and led me from one cell to another. He was the one with a flash of guilt across his eyes when I wouldn't cooperate and help them trick the other girls.

"Please," I whispered, shuffling my way along the wall, well aware I had nowhere to go. *"Please don't."*

One of their weapons was pushed through the bars, and Sol shrieked when they prodded him with it. His back spasmed, and he collapsed to his knees again.

"Fuck her, Sol. Your life may depend on it."

Pitifully, he stared up at me, and although I could hear my heart pounding, I held his eye contact.

He doesn't want to hurt me.

The thought seemed pathetic when he stood again, and while his first few steps were shaky, he soon regained himself and strode purposefully over to me before he backed me against the wall. The jeering got louder, and I turned my head away and squeezed my eyes shut as the tears started to fall. Sol's fingers grazed the inside of my thigh, and I clenched my legs closed as the laughter outside the cell increased.

"Misha." I opened my eyes a crack as Sol spoke, and I looked at him out of the corner of my eye, my jaw clenched and body shaking. "I don't want to hurt you."

"Let me guess," I whispered, barely keeping my teeth from chattering. "This will be a lot easier if I cooperate."

Sol looked as though my words had hurt him when I hissed them out, but I didn't care. I turned my head away and squeezed my eyes shut again.

His hand brushed over my shoulder, a lackluster movement without malice or passion, but I shuddered anyway. What he was about to do wasn't right, whether or not his movements were mechanical.

I screamed as a bolt of electricity shot through Sol's hand, where he touched me, and I opened my eyes to see the group retracting the weapon through the bars. They'd shocked Sol while he touched me, and I'd received secondhand pain from it. The skin on my face felt seared, and I winced, wondering the full extent of the pain Sol was feeling if that's what it felt like to receive only a taste of it.

"Look at him, flaccid." There was laughter, and Sol dropped his chin to his chest. "Let's leave the lovers alone for the night. Maybe he'll be able to get it up without an audience."

I relaxed slightly, and Sol pulled away from me. Before the group left, they shocked Sol with the weapon again, and this time, he collapsed to his knees before covering his face with his hands. "Make it happen overnight, Sol," one of them jeered, gripping the bars and rattling them menacingly. "Or tomorrow, we'll strap her down and make sure it happens."

They left, and I slid down the wall until I hit the floor, letting my legs stretch out in front of me.

"Why are they doing this?" I whispered, my head still tilted to the side, staring at the door where the group of Ghaal had disappeared. I wasn't expecting an answer, so when I looked up, a hollow chuckle emanated from Sol.

"They are punishing me," he replied.

I stared into his eyes, jumping slightly when he blinked, his eyelids closing in from the sides instead of from the top and bottom. Sol pushed himself to his feet, and I tensed before he walked to the opposite side of the cell and sat as far from me as he could get.

"You don't want to hurt me." I'm not sure if I was asking, hoping, or trying to convince him, but he met my gaze and shook his head.

"No."

"Why are you in here with me?"

Something passed across his face then, and I tilted my head, taking him in. It was easy to see them only as an alien species when they were capturing and hurting me, but watching him like this, closer than I wanted to be, I could see the nuances of his expressions and the similarities between us. "Don't hate me for what I am."

"I don't hate you," I said automatically, a response I couldn't control, but I realized it was true a moment later. I didn't *hate* Sol specifically. "I'm afraid of you."

He nodded and turned away. "I don't blame you."

"What did you do? Why are they punishing you?" I was going to keep asking because the fact he hadn't already told me made me think there was something he didn't *want* to tell me.

"Because I released your friend after they captured her."

I sat bolt upright, and my head spun with thoughts and the motion. Before I knew it, I was leaning forward and had pressed my hands against the cool floor, wanting to know more but afraid to get closer. "What? Who? Tell me what happened." I couldn't keep the desperation from my voice. There was no pretending I was stronger than I was when it came to protecting the others. I could try to hold my own and keep my tears back while they questioned me, but the idea of the other girls falling into the hands of the Ghaal had my arms shaking as I leaned toward Sol. "Tell me."

He sighed. "I suppose it doesn't matter if I tell you. They're punishing me by being in here, and when they eventually lose interest in torturing me, they'll kill me." I said nothing and waited for him to continue, "They captured another human female in the forest. She had dark hair like you, not black but dark." He studied me for a moment. "But it was longer and tied into braids."

"Erica," I breathed out her name, then slapped my hands over my mouth as I realized what I'd done. I didn't want to give *any* information to the Ghaal, not even Sol.

He chuckled again. "I won't tell them anything...

your names make little difference anyway." Before I could speak again, he cut me off. "She is with a Synth, so don't worry about her. I'm sure he'll protect her with his life now she's been taken once."

"You trust the Synths?"

He huffed out another humorless laugh. "More than my own kind." His eyes were pleading when he looked at me again. "You must understand, female, I don't wish for our species to die off, but the methods they are using as they grow more desperate... I wonder if we would be better off dead."

"But if you're feeling this way, perhaps others are too."

"Funny, your friend said the same thing." He tilted his head. "No, female, I do not think so, hence..." he gestured around the cell, "... I am here and not rescued by some rebellious group."

"Are the other girls... are they..." I trailed off, unable to ask in case I didn't want to know the answer.

"You are the only one of your lot they have at this time," he said, and it was like a lead weight had been lifted from my chest, and I could breathe again.

"What happens tomorrow? When they realize overnight we haven't... will they use..." I swallowed and couldn't help but picture things as the questions ran through my mind. "Will they use machines on me to get me pregnant?"

"We are superstitious beings, female. You're safe until they have all six of you."

My brows drew together. "Six? There's only four of us."

"Not four, six." His eyes flickered to the circles in the wall above my head, where the blue light glowed across the cell. "Always in sixes, six is a sacred number. There are six Synths. Six points on the star of our uniforms..." he held my stare as my eyes widened. "Six human females."

Scrambling to my feet, I cupped my palms around my eyes and squinted against the light. I'd assumed these were simply light sources, but as I blinked past the glow's intensity, I realized they were windows into small chambers.

My conversation with Sahcor ran through my mind.

What if we weren't the first humans?

My eyes adjusted to the light, and she finally came into shape—a human woman, her eyes closed and long lashes over her cheeks, hair flowing around her face as if underwater. But there was no motion—she was frozen in time. I hastily moved to the next window—another woman. The blue light made it difficult to tell what color their hair was, but it seemed light-colored, I'd guess. Not that it mattered. The second woman was movie-star beautiful, her full lips parted slightly as though in a peaceful slumber.

But she wasn't peaceful—she was captured like me.

How long had they been here?

Did they even know they'd been taken?

Heart hammering against the inside of my chest, I dropped back to the floor, tucked my legs underneath me, and struggled to keep myself together.

They only took four of us because they already had two.

They *already had two.*

Were there more?

"Dead," Sol said, his tone hollow, and I looked up at him as I fought to keep my tears at bay. "These two were brought to us in a group of six and are all who remain. The other four were killed when the Ghaal, in their haste and excitement at finding a match, wanted to make *absolutely sure.* With what lingering technology we had, they cut the women open, and none of them survived the surgery. They tried to salvage their wombs..." He shuddered, and my stomach churned.

What they must have gone through.

"How long?" I choked out.

"How long have they been in stasis? Years, eight at least, maybe more." He shook his head. "They wanted four more before they started again. They want to have six."

"Me... my friends..."

"Yes." When I looked at Sol, his eyes were full of emotion and resignation. He had no real fight left in him, and I curled further into myself, wondering if he would give in and take me to stop the torture.

I shook my head. "All their technology, such an advanced race..." I turned to him, holding his gaze for as long as I could before turning back to face the bars, "... and superstitions still hold them back?" It was my turn to huff out a laugh without humor. "Perhaps I should be thankful... it's the only thing keeping me safe from them tonight."

CHAPTER 25

MISHA

Sleep didn't come easy, and what short naps I caught were the product of sheer exhaustion. Propped up in the corner of the cell, I had curled into myself as much as possible against the chill of the night. The winds outside roared and sent an icy breeze through the bars. Sol was shuffling around in the opposite corner, no doubt trying to sleep as well. I was almost desperate enough for warmth that I considered going to him and hunkering down, but the scent of his skin reminded me of the other Ghaal, and I couldn't shake the fear. The fact he hadn't attacked me and helped Erica were two points I held on to, but they were no good against a flood of fear.

Besides, I only had his word to go on that he'd helped Erica.

This could be another trap.

The light from the sun was inviting against my face, and I slowly opened my eyes, wanting to keep them closed for a moment longer to relish in the warmth and perhaps to pretend I wasn't in this cell. But having my eyes closed also made me vulnerable.

When I rolled so I was sitting facing the cell bars, Sol was already awake and crouched in the corner watching me. He steered his gaze from my face when I caught him staring.

"I'm sorry," he said.

I gave an automatic answer. "For what?"

"For staring. I can tell it makes you uncomfortable."

I almost snorted. "You staring at me is the least of my discomfort, Sol."

He pulled a face as if he wasn't sure if he should laugh or despair.

When the main door opened to the hall outside my cell, Sol and I scrambled to our feet and pressed our backs against the rear of the cell.

"How was he, human? Did you get off with his cock inside you?"

I grit my teeth and ignored the whirlwind of

responses I could come back with, all of which would probably result in another shock from the weapons each of them held. They turned their attention to Sol, and he held their stares.

"I don't think he did it, Xra."

"I think you're right. Maybe he needs more encouragement."

They lifted their weapons but stopped when the hall door slid open again, and a third Ghaal entered. "Enough. We have plans for her first."

"Whatever you say, Rah."

The first two Ghaal backed off immediately and stepped to the side, allowing Rah to hover his hand over the ball that unlocked the cell. The door creaked open, and the two smaller Ghaal sprang into action, one of them brandishing their weapon at Sol, the other at me.

"Stay here, Sol. We'll bring her back soon, and you can try again."

"You," the one called Rah snapped at me. I jerked my head toward him and away from Sol's gaze as the Ghaal jabbed his finger toward me and then the door. "Out."

Keeping myself pressed to the outside of the cell, I worked around the corners, trying to put as much distance between the Ghaals who held the weapons and me. When I reached the cell door, Rah grabbed my arm, a tight grip that was immediately painful. "If you run, I won't chase you." He sneered and glanced back at his comrades as they locked Sol in the cell again. "But *they* will, along with every other male you encounter."

Gritting my teeth until my jaw hurt, I held his eye contact, said nothing, and tripped over my feet as he jerked me forward before I followed them out of the hall.

"Your Synth came for you last night," Rah said calmly, chuckling when I tensed under his grip, unable to stop the reaction. "He killed one of the guards but didn't get much further than that." He tutted. "I'm advocating for the Synths not to be killed. Not yet. I still think they may be useful. Deep down, they are animals designed for breeding, and I'm going to put forward to the lab the idea of stringing you up, legs spread and naked, then torturing you and the Synth until he's in a rage. Get his instincts going, and he may not be able to stop himself from taking you."

I was shaking but refused to speak. Sahcor wouldn't do that to me... *would he?* The Ghaal knew more about his genetic makeup than I did. Could he really be tortured to the point of no return until he broke, and instinct took over? I wanted to believe it wasn't true, but Rah glanced at me almost gleefully as if he could read my thoughts.

As if he knew for sure what the Synths were capable of.

Swallowing back my tears, I cleared my throat

and stared straight ahead as we entered a lab.

I knew there was no use in fighting, but there wasn't anything that could stop my instincts from raging for freedom when I was grabbed and held down in a chair as clamps were closed over my arms and legs, pinning me in place. The metal was cold against my skin, but it wasn't the only thing that had me shivering. I was held in a sitting position, and I clung to the information Sol had provided me—that I was safe from any real attempts to impregnate me until they had all the girls together.

But still, they had tried to force Sol to take me last night. What was really stopping them from *having a little fun* while they waited for the other girls to be captured? The Ghaal seemed a strained combination of patient and desperate. The trick they pulled, allowing me to be rescued last time, was a gamble. On the one hand, they seemed content to wait, while on the other, they clung to our existence on this planet as the savior of their species.

A lump formed in my throat as my thoughts collated.

That was just it, wasn't it? We had nowhere to go. Not really.

We couldn't leave the planet and could only cover distances we could reach by walking. They *had us*—the girls and I were here for the taking.

Their desperation in having us kidnapped from Earth dissipated now we were here, and they could wait us out. They could take weeks, months even, to trick and lure us until we were all together. Even if they didn't have the technology to simply capture us, they seemed capable of luring us in.

We had nowhere to run.

When a cold tool was pressed against my arm, I tried to jerk away and caused the stinging cool of the metal restraints to dig into my skin. The tool made an unpleasant scratching noise as a clamp shot out and secured itself around my arm.

"What are you doing?" My question ended with an anguished squeak I couldn't help.

"Relax." Nothing was relaxing about the Ghaal's voice holding the tool to my arm. "This is just going to monitor your vitals to make sure you're healthy when it comes to insemination."

I didn't care. I didn't want it in my arm or my body. Struggling did nothing, and my breathing was labored by the time the thick needle pierced my skin, creating a searing pain that made me scream. It wasn't like getting a shot, the needle moving back and forth in my arm for far too long. When it retracted, there was another scratchy noise, following a burn that cut my scream off until my mouth was hanging open in a silent cry for help.

Tears streamed down my face as the tool was removed, and I cast a weary glance at my arm, noting the thin red line where the wound had been sealed. I wanted to claw whatever it was inside me out, to tear the wound open and yank the thing free. But as the restraints were removed from my arms and legs, I went limp in the Ghaals' arms as I was dragged back to my cell. All the fight sucked from me as my body recovered from the pain.

My legs collapsed when I was thrown into my cell, and I crawled into the corner, ignoring Sol's quiet call of my name, and drifted into an uneasy and exhausted sleep.

My head throbbed as I woke, my forehead pressing against my knees. Sighing, I stayed in that position and wrapped my arms tighter around my legs.

"Female?" Sol's call was tentative, quiet, and gentle, everything I didn't associate with the Ghaal. I didn't lift my head, only sighed again before humming so he knew I'd heard him. "Are you okay?"

"Peachy."

"I don't understand."

I huffed out a laugh, not feeling any desire to smile. "Not really, Sol."

"I am sorry for everything."

"It's not your fault."

I heard him shuffling across the floor as he moved closer to where I sat, the sound halting when I stiffened. "I took part with the other females, all sorts of species. I'm not blameless. And I'm sorry."

I couldn't even bring myself to utter the standard response—*it's okay.*

Because it *wasn't* okay.

It was very fucking far from okay.

Everything they'd done, everything the other girls and I had been through, was that something that could be repented through words alone? Sol said he was in here with me because he had helped Erica escape, but was that enough? I didn't trust him, not like I trusted Sahcor. Even though my bond with Sahcor started as one of necessity, I felt no such similar inclination to forge the same connection with Sol. I appreciate he didn't rape me, but that's as far as it went.

Where was Sahcor?

Rah had mentioned he didn't want to kill the Synths—not yet, at least—and I'm certain Sahcor would be attempting to rescue me. But what would the Ghaal do to stop him? Would they hurt him?

Lifting my head, I stared out through the bars. There were no guards that I could see, but no doubt there were many outside the doors and building waiting for Sahcor, perhaps even hoping I would make a run for it so they could chase me down.

"How long was I out?"

"Not long. Less than an hour. It's still morning."

Sighing again, I stretched my arms above my head and winced when the sting of the implant brought with it the stark reminder I had alien technology under my skin. Pressing my fingers to the wound, I could almost roll the implant under my skin, about the size of a medicine capsule.

"Do you have a knife?" I asked. It was a stupid question. Of course, they wouldn't let Sol have a weapon, but I needed this thing out of me. *Now.*

"You can't cut it out. It's fused to your muscle. You'll damage your tendons if you try."

"I don't care. I want it out."

"Female…"

I was on my feet before I had time to register my actions and strode across the cell floor to meet Sol halfway. Jabbing my finger against his chest, he raised his hands in surrender. "My name is *Misha,* okay? *Misha.* Enough of this *female* crap. I'm more than just a body. Although none of you assholes give a damn about that."

He weakly tried to protest when I stormed to the bars, ignoring the cold burn as I grabbed them and shook. "I want this fucking thing *out of my body!*"

The bars rattled, and the smallest click betrayed them when there was a shift. Pausing, I held my breath, certain I had misheard. Flexing my fingers around the bars, I slowly slid the door to the side, gasping when it shuddered and then moved.

It was unlocked.

"Misha…" Sol's voice was full of warning as he took a step away from the door. My eyes widened as I slid it open further, revealing an exit where I could simply stroll through. "It's a trap."

"I know." I didn't look at Sol and kept my gaze straight ahead at my perceived and perhaps impossible freedom. "I know."

Licking my lips, I stepped back. Every nerve in my body was screaming for me to run from this place. While the logical part of my mind which was still functioning under the fear and stress, I knew Sol was right and this was a trap, but my fingers twitched at my side as I itched to simply run.

Run.

"I have to try," I whispered.

Sol was right behind me, and it was a testament to how distracted I was that I didn't move away from him. He didn't touch me, though I'm certain in any other circumstance, he would have put his hand on my shoulder or perhaps dramatically spun me around to face him to convince me not to do what I was thinking of doing. "This was no accident, Misha. Please."

"I know. I know." Reaching up, I rubbed my temples. "I'm not an idiot, Sol. I know this is a trap. But…"

But *what?*

But what if I make it?

But what if it *wasn't* a trap?

But what if Sahcor is waiting for me?

A weight dropped in my stomach at the thought of Sahcor. I desperately wanted to go back to him. But Rah's threat about using the Synths echoed in my mind. If I took this chance, not only could I not try to find the girls, I'd also have to stay away from Sahcor. I was as much of a danger to him as I was to the others. I could run as far and as fast as I could. I knew just enough about this place, and now I think I could survive.

And the other girls, they'd be safe.

Until they had all six.

My throat closed up as I held back the emotion. Sahcor would think I'd abandoned him and didn't care for him. I could only hope he'd understand.

Still, without turning around, I said, "Thank you for your apology, Sol, and for what you did to help save Erica."

"Misha—"

"You should take this chance, too, while you can. They'll chase me before they chase you."

With that, I stepped over the cell's threshold, pausing for only a moment for retribution that didn't come before I bolted down the hall.

CHAPTER 26

SAHCOR

The day dragged out.

Night would be my best chance at rescuing Misha, but doing nothing all day while I waited for nightfall was tearing me apart. I fished, cooked, and gathered plants and treats. I gathered more seaweed to dry and filled the water bags to stock up my cave so when I had Misha back, we didn't have to leave for days. We could stay safe and close together, and when we used up all the stock I had gathered, then I would take her farther away. I'd swim around the coast with Misha clinging to my back, farther and farther from the Ghaal, until we found a new cave somewhere to make a home together.

Keeping busy wasn't enough to stop my mind from racing.

By early afternoon, I found myself loitering around the rocky outcrops that led to the Ghaal colony. I kept to the ocean. It was easier to keep out of sight from any sentries if I could quickly duck underwater and move faster than I could on foot.

Even the motion of the water carrying my body with its tides wasn't enough to keep me calm, the animal that lived beneath my skin was more than aware my mate was in trouble. A complete animal would have rampaged into the colony already, and I probably would have died trying to get to her. Thankfully, I had barely enough control to realize I needed to wait and plan my attack. The fewer Ghaal I encountered, the better, and if I could get in and out without being seen, that would be the ideal situation.

Although judging by last night, that may not be possible.

Movement caught my eye, and I stilled, hovering so my line of sight was just above the water's surface, and I'd be almost invisible to any onlookers.

The movement wasn't on the beach but on top of the cliff face, the bushes shuddering as a figure skittered from one to another.

A glint of sunlight off dark red hair caught my attention as I focused on the pale skin of the figure, partially covered by clothes made of dried weeds.

I snarled.

Misha.

But she wasn't moving toward the beach back to me. Was she lost? Or had she intentionally climbed away from where she knew she could find me?

I lost sight of her as she moved farther inland. Unable to contain the growl that rumbled through my chest, I moved toward the shore before heading straight for the rocks to climb to find her.

Climbing was difficult. My skin was not adapted to survive and excel when it came to the harsh edges of the rocks, and my webbed fingers and feet didn't assist when I needed additional grip.

But I pushed myself forward.

My fingers slipped in the soil when I reached the top, and I heaved my body onto the flat surface. Without giving myself time to rest, I was on my feet and tracked Misha from her scent and the small trail of destruction she'd left behind her—bent bushes, trampled grasses, and the interested caw of a volti that flew circles above us. They'd be attracted by her movement, but she was too big of a meal for them. At least she was safe from the volti.

Still unsure why Misha would be running from me, I kept my movements as silent as I could, darting between trees and bushes until I found her weaving her way through the scattered trees of the scarce woodlands. Tilting my head, I watched her for a moment. The sun that shone off her cheeks showed she'd been crying, her skin red, flushed, and streaked with dried tears. Now and then, her breath would be interrupted with a quiet sob, but she kept moving.

I followed.

Aside from scratches on her legs and arms, she seemed unharmed—at least physically. I had no idea what had happened to her while in the colony or how she had managed to escape.

But she should have no reason to run from me.

She *must* know that.

Darting out from behind the trees, Misha turned at the sound of my pounding feet, gasping and backing up a few steps hastily as I approached. When she tripped, I was there to catch her and lowered her to the ground under me as she started sobbing harder and beat her fists weakly against my chest.

"My mate, I'm here." I tried to calm her, whispering soothing words and brushing her hair back. "It's me, Sahcor. Do not be afraid."

"You can't be here," Misha sobbed, still trying to press against my chest, but the attempts were feeble and without passion. "You need to leave me alone. You're not safe with me."

My brows pulled together. "I don't understand."

"*Please,*" she pleaded with me. Her sobbing subsided as she met my eyes, although tears still ran freely down her cheeks and fell onto the soil beneath her. "Please leave. They'll find you. They'll find me, and then they'll kill you. I can't lose... I can't be the reason... you have to be safe."

Misha had stopped fighting me now and laid limply under me as I supported my weight above her. Dropping onto one elbow, I ran my fingers down her cheek. Misha hiccupped and tilted her head into my touch. "My mate..." I whispered. I wanted to understand, but she had been through so very much. I didn't want to push her, but I had to know. "Do you despise me?"

"*No.*" Her cry was sudden and loud as if she desperately needed me to believe her words were true, and her eyes widened as she met my gaze. "I don't hate you. I *love* you."

She gasped, and I blinked at her. The words seemed significant to her, and I didn't understand that either. *Of course,* I loved her. Did she not know that? She was my mate. I wanted a family with her.

"Misha, please." My voice cracked, and she hiccupped again. "Please help me to understand.

You say you love me, yet you run from me."

"Oh, Sahcor." All energy had faded from her as she closed her eyes. I stroked her hair again, and a growl started in my chest when she sighed and let me continue, "The Ghaal. They said they were going to capture and torture you until you went crazy. Then string me up, so you would…" She swallowed. Bitterness, rage, and fear mingled in her voice until the feel of the words was sour. "They said you were still the best DNA they had, so why not use you… use all your brothers."

When I sighed, she reached up, curled her fingers into my hair, and gripped it until I looked at her.

"Don't you see, Sahcor? They let me go the first time as bait for the girls and again this time to try again. They want all of us girls together, and if they get you and your brothers, too, that only sweetens the deal for them." When she dropped her hands from me, she pushed herself to her elbows and tried to shuffle out from underneath me. "I can't be near you, or them, or anyone. I'm a danger to you all. You have to let me go."

With a snarl, I grabbed the front of her top, my fingers curling around the weeds and brushing against the delicate flesh of her breasts. Misha's eyes widened as I tugged her down, forcing her back under me before I caged her in with my arms and dropped my weight so she was pinned.

"I'm not letting you leave," I growled out.

"You have to… they won't stop. They won't ever stop."

"If you don't want to find the girls, that's okay. We'll run away together, but I'm not leaving you to be alone. You need me, and I… I need you."

"Sahcor…" she whispered, her face screwed up with pain. "You're making this harder."

"Misha…" I waited for her to meet my eyes. "Tell me you don't want to be with me, and I'll leave."

"You know I want to be with you."

"So, let's run. Together."

Her pupils darted back and forth as if unable to focus on one part of my face. She was searching for a reason to say no, looking for an excuse for me to let her go, but her putting me in danger wasn't enough of a reason. Misha was safer with me, and I would do everything and anything to protect her. We'd find a new place to call our own.

We'd be safe together.

"Do you want me?" I asked.

Misha stilled, her mind running over itself as every thought and emotion tripped over each other and every thought displayed in her shifting expression. I stroked her cheek again to ground her and remind her that it was only her and me here.

Tentatively, her leg came around my calf, and she gave me an encouraging pull toward her. I complied, pressed the hard length of my cock between her legs, and rubbed once. Misha whined quietly, her hips lifting to meet mine.

"I want you," she said. This time, when she tangled her fingers in my hair, it was to bring my lips to hers.

The growling started anew. Misha moaned into my mouth as I pressed down against her, and all the fear she had been leaving me because she hated or was angry at me dissipated. The weight from my chest lifted, and I tangled my fingers into Misha's hair, pushed my tongue into her mouth, and groaned when she welcomed me and ran her tongue against mine.

"Sahcor," she gasped out and pulled her lips away as her legs tugged me closer. "I'm sorry, I was trying to do the right thing—"

I silenced her with a kiss. "I know, Misha. I know you because we are the same. I'm only thankful you don't hate me."

"I could never..." She punctuated each word with another kiss on my face. "*Never*. Hate. You."

Our lips met again in a clash of desperation, and I held her tighter against me. Misha's legs parted, inviting me in. I thrust forward and groaned at the sensation of my cock sliding between her cunt's wet lips. Angling my hips, I pressed forward while Misha lifted her hips to meet my thrust, and my cock sank deep into her warm cunt.

"Fuck, Sahcor." Her moans made my cock twitch as I pushed inside her, her small thighs spreading further. "Fuck me."

I wasted no time, plunging my cock deep into her before pulling out and doing it again. I wasn't going to let her go, not ever. I held inside a deep hatred for myself. Misha had been taken when she should have been safe with me. At every turn, I've done her wrong, and yet she still parts her legs for me, her cunt squeezing my cock so perfectly. I needed to do better. If we were going to have a family, if Misha were truly to accept me as her mate and have our child, then she needed to be able to rely on me to protect her.

I had to do better.

For my mate.

"Misha," I whispered, and her moans were gasps against my ear as I pulled her closer.

"Sahcor?"

"I won't let you down again."

"Wh-what?" Her fingers were through my hair again, her eyes closed, and her head titled back in ecstasy.

"You've been in danger because I've failed to protect you."

"Is this... *fuck...*" After another thrust, she gasped again, her fingers tugging against my hair. "Is this really the time to talk about it?"

"I've failed you."

Her fingers curled into my hair and tugged hard until I grunted and met her eyes. At the same time, she wrapped her legs around my waist, her skirt hiking up to her stomach as she halted my movements inside her by gripping me with her thighs. "Sahcor, I trust you."

"Maybe you shouldn't. I don't want you alone, but I have failed you."

A smile ghosted across her lips. "I'm staying with you, okay? You said you wanted me to stay. We'll be together, just you and me, and we'll find somewhere safe to be." Her smile dropped as her expression tightened. "Being taken by the Ghaal was my own fault, not yours. I felt something was off, but I ignored my instincts. It won't happen again." The harsh tug against my hair turned into a caress as she pressed her lips against mine, and her thighs tightened around me. "But can we please talk about this when you're not balls deep inside me?"

My lip twitched into a smirk. "Okay, my mate."

Her chuckle morphed into another moan as I ground my hips against her, making sure her sensitive clit was stimulated with each rub until her cries reached a new pitch. I found a rhythm, forcing her closer to her peak as she squeezed around me. This was a new beginning for us, and I would do better by Misha. My brothers would be ashamed of me for how I had let my mate come to harm more than once. Once was too many.

Growling, I pushed down the hatred that rose in my throat again. Now was not the time.

My Misha needed to come.

Harder. Faster.

Until she gaped against my ear. "Sahcor... gonna come..."

The sound was so sweet, and as she squeezed tight around my cock, I clamped a hand over her mouth to muffle the sound of her pleasure-filled screams. The act felt unnatural, but soon we would find a new place to live, where I could spend the day with my mouth on her cunt, making her scream as she came over and over. Thrusting harder into her, I gripped her hip and held her still as she whimpered and moaned around my hand.

When I came, I pushed inside her harder, determined for her to take all my seed, for it to push into her womb and make her round with my child.

Our child.

As I lowered on top of her, touching as much of her body as possible with mine without having her bear my weight, Misha's fingers traced down my back in lazy patterns as my cock twitched inside her.

"Sahcor?"

I hummed against her shoulder, and Misha squirmed at the sensation.

"What do we do now?"

"We go back to my cave so you can rest, then we'll leave and find a new place to live."

"Far from the Ghaal?" I'm sure she knew the

answer to that, but still, she asked with a hint of trepidation. The thought twisted my stomach into knots. Misha didn't feel as safe with me as she should, and fear still gripped every part of her at the dangers on this planet.

I would fix that.

"Far from everything."

CHAPTER
27

MISHA

"I don't want to do this, Misha."

I pushed the knife against his palm harder when he didn't wrap his fingers around it. "You have to."

While I hated the pain in his eyes at the idea of hurting me, I wanted this alien technology *out of my body* right *now.* It had already been in there too long. I didn't trust I had the strength—physically or the willpower—to do it myself. My body would rebel against the pain I knew would come, and I would stop cutting. There was no anesthetic or numbing cream.

I'd just had to grit my teeth and bear it.

But the alternative was leaving this damn thing inside me, and I also hated the idea of that.

Sahcor had a steady hand and could make a more precise cut while I gripped onto something and bit down on a piece of wood to stop from screaming.

"Misha, you don't understand." He limply held the bone knife in his hand, and the slightest movement would knock it from his barely-there grip. "You've come to so much harm already because of me, I can't... I can't hurt you intentionally."

My lips pursed with determination even as I felt the emotion swell in my eyes. Mentally, I went over everything that had happened since I'd landed on this planet. The initial abduction by the Moeks was nothing to do with Sahcor, but when the Ghaal took me, wasn't I already heading toward their colony anyway without Sahcor's help? Granted, tying me up wasn't the best way to go about helping me, but he'd explained to me that he was responding to instincts and urges that hadn't surfaced in years. He was an intelligent being who had been living like an animal, putting aside anything that could resemble his desires and wants to help others. Then, *I* stirred everything up.

I couldn't blame him for that. I only remembered how he rescued me.

Then I almost drowned, and as I watched Sahcor's eyes, I could see the pain swimming there as if he, too, was remembering everything he saw as a failure. The giant fish thing that tried to drag me to my death—the maasi—Sahcor didn't see them as a threat because he was too big for them to attack.

An oversight? Yes. Avoidable? Absolutely.

But we'd both been thrown into a situation where we figured it out as we went. How I would react to this environment and how the environment would react to me was as much of a mystery for Sahcor as it was for me.

Then being taken by the Ghaal again. That was all on me.

I *knew* something was wrong. My gut was churning when I heard the cry for help, and a small voice screamed in the back of my mind to wait for Sahcor. But I acted anyway and recklessly. I could subdue these thoughts by telling myself I was acting rashly because I thought one of the girls was in danger and wanted to help them. But there were a million questions I could have asked or things I could have done to make sure the situation wasn't a trap. I was smarter than that—I think things through again and again, and it was what I usually did. I'd always wanted to think I was the sort of person who would get into an emergency situation and leap into action, but apparently, that's not how I dealt with things, and it was a rude slap in the face to realize.

I didn't blame Sahcor. He had repeatedly saved

me, and then come after me when I was again trying to do what I thought was best, but looking back, was foolish.

Staying away from the girls, yes. But staying away from Sahcor made no sense.

We'd be together, far from here.

"We've both made mistakes," I said, starting slowly. There was no way I could tell Sahcor not to blame himself because he would anyway. The best thing I could do was reassure him that *I* didn't hold him responsible. "But I don't blame you for anything that's happened to me. I'm safer with you than I am with anyone. I know you don't want to hurt me, but *this...*" I pressed on where the implant was, rolling it around under my skin for emphasis, "... is Ghaal technology. I don't care that it's only to monitor my vitals or whatever so I can get pregnant faster. I want it *out.*" I grabbed Sahcor's face. Once again, he hadn't said a word, instead falling into one of those silences where I could almost see his mind working a thousand miles a minute. "I know it'll pain you to do this, but you're the only one I trust."

Sahcor's fingers closed around the blade as the muscles in his jaw tensed. He didn't say a word, and he didn't need to. I nodded sharply, dropped myself onto the cave floor, and leaned against the smooth wall, hoping the coolness would soothe me, even though I was already sweating from the knowledge of the impending pain. Grabbing a handful of the dried seaweed I'd knotted up earlier, I placed it between my teeth, biting down and glancing at Sahcor as I nodded again.

He kneeled next to me, grabbed my arm, and pressed his thumb hard under the location of the implant. I braced myself for him to start, knowing he often doesn't talk when he gets like this. But when I opened my eyes, he was staring at me. "I make no promises, Misha," he said, his jaw tense. "But for you, I'll try."

Pressing my lips together, I turned my head away as he lowered the tip of the knife to my arm. The sharp prick of the blade as it broke my skin made me jump, and I twisted my free hand into the nearby bedding, trying to keep still. I groaned as he cut deeper, sweat coming on my forehead and mingling with the tears on my cheeks as it dripped. There was only so long I could hold back the screams of pain, and soon I was writhing and crying, unable to stop my body's reaction in its attempts to get away from the pain.

"It's not going to work, Misha. It's embedded in your muscle somehow."

"Deeper!" I screamed, dropping the weeds from between my teeth.

Sahcor worked the blade for more agonizing seconds, and just when I thought I was going to pass out, spots of gray popped into my vision as a rush of warmth swarmed up my neck. He stopped. The blade was dropped, and his hand slapped a concoction of herbs over my arm he'd prepared in advance.

"Did you get it?" I panted as gray swam in the edges of my vision, slowly clearing. Sahcor didn't answer and worked steadily to wrap the wound on my arm as my blood dripped onto the cave floor. "Sahcor! Did you get it?"

He spoke through gritted teeth, "No."

"What?" I tried to shift to face him, but the sudden movement caused my vision to darken as my head spun. Leaning back against the wall, I placed a hand on my forehead, not prepared for how slick my skin was with sweat. "Why did you stop?"

"It's too deep, Misha. It's embedded right in the muscle. You'll pass out if I get it out or lose too much blood. I can't do it."

"Can't or won't?" I hated that it was still in me, and right now, that anger was being directed toward Sahcor.

"Both!" He snarled at me then, a long, drawn-out sound that dissipated into a harsh growl as he tied off the makeshift bandage on my arm with a jerk. Eyes widening, I stilled. Sahcor didn't rage like this, not at me, and the change in demeanor was startling. When his green eyes met mine, they were blazing bright, intense with anger, fear, and everything I'd felt over the past few weeks compounded into a single moment. "I made no promises. I told you I would try, but I will *not* risk your life while you scream and lose consciousness."

"Sahcor—"

"We will *not* be trying again. *I can't lose you again!*"

We stilled then, and my hand came up to tentatively clamp over the covering on my arm. I looked at the floor. "I'm sorry."

Sahcor slumped back and dropped his weight heavily to the cave floor before he sat cross-legged. "No. No, Misha. You have nothing to be sorry for. I'm sorry. Once again, I failed you."

I huffed through my nose. "Because you wouldn't do as I asked and tear my muscles open? I don't think you have to be sorry for that."

He lifted his gaze to mine. "I only want what's best for you."

"I know." Leaning forward, I crawled to close the space between us, keeping my bandaged arm folded against my body. Sahcor's eyes didn't leave the spot where he'd cut until I kneeled next to him, cupping his cheek in my palm. "I know."

When his eyes found mine, we stared at each other in silence again, and I realized how incredibly intimate I had become with Sahcor in such a short time. Not just the sex but a physical and emotional intimacy I hadn't allowed myself before. The simple touches—brushes of our hands, fingers to lips, and palms to cheeks—were things I didn't even think about with him and didn't second-guess. The texture of his skin was a comfort now—something about how different we were while somehow being the same felt like two puzzle pieces that, despite being galaxies apart, were meant to fit together.

"Will you hold me?" I asked, already knowing the answer but needing to hear it from him. Because all I needed was him. "While we sleep?"

His brows furrowed for just a moment as if he couldn't figure out why I was asking. Whether he understood or simply chose to accept it as something I had to verbalize, I didn't know.

Sahcor's fingers brushed through my hair and pushed it from my face as he passed through a few knots. "Always."

We slept deeply, and in the morning, Sahcor didn't need to hunt as he had already gathered supplies. Sahcor wanted me to rest in the cave for a few days before we started looking for a new home, but I didn't want to wait. We could return to his cave at night, but at the very least, I wanted to spend the days seeing what else was out there.

So, we swam, or more specifically, Sahcor swam,

and I clung to him. He skimmed along gracefully just below the surface, coming up at regular intervals so I could take a deep breath. We found a rhythm like that, and a sense of pure freedom gripped my heart.

I was one with Sahcor and this place. *Finally.*

Later in the day, Sahcor removed the bandages, using the seawater to wash away what was left of the mixture he'd packed into the wound. The cut had scabbed over but was far from healed. At least it wasn't an open wound anymore. I hated that I could still see a small bump slightly to the side of the cut as if it had shifted after we'd tried to get it out. I couldn't care less if I had a scar, but I didn't want to see that little lump reminding me every day that I had Ghaal technology inside me.

"We should rewrap the wound," Sahcor said, dragging me from my thoughts as I met his gaze.

"Later." Tentatively, I dipped the wound below the ocean's surface. It didn't sting. If anything, the cool water had a pleasant tingling effect on it. "Let it breathe."

We swam, and Sahcor hunted fresh fish and brought food back to me.

Although he kept very close by, even when fishing.

Treading water, I accepted pieces of fish as Sahcor handed them to me. "Do you want a cave on the land or partially out to sea?"

I thought, popping the meat in my mouth. "Out to

sea, I think. I like that we need to go underwater to get to your current cave... maybe something like that."

Sahcor turned and looked out into the distance, no doubt seeing things I couldn't. "There isn't another peninsula for a long way. Several days' journey."

"That's fine." Sahcor turned back to me, and I watched the purple glow of the curious markings on his body move under the water. I smiled. "Why does that surprise you? Further away is better, I think." My smile dropped as realization hit. "Oh, Sahcor, I'm sorry. You've lived in that cave for so long, and I'm talking about leaving like it's nothing."

With a smooth motion, he swept toward me, dropping the fish bones into the water. I watched as they drifted down until they were obscured by the depth. "I'm happy as long as I am with you."

"How corny." I chuckled at his expression and kissed him quickly on his lips as I threw my arms around his neck. When he stiffened under my touch, I laughed. "Was the kiss that bad?" Sahcor didn't move, his gaze fixed on a point in the distance.

Something was wrong, and my stomach churned around our recent meal. "What? What is it? What's wrong?"

"There's something different in the water," he said.

"What do you mean?" It was difficult not to panic.

If Sahcor was spooked, then I was fucking terrified. "What do you mean *something different?*"

"Human."

For a moment, I wasn't sure if I'd heard him correctly. "Human?"

"Same shape as you. Swimming near the shore not far from here." He tensed again as if his body was reacting to the water's vibrations. I couldn't sense anything beyond the lazy rise and fall of the gentle waves, too far from the shore to be caught in the crash as they turned over.

"Take me to the shore. Then go check it out."

"I'm not leaving you alone."

I stared him down. "I'm not sure I want to see the other girls or have them see me, okay? But you need to make sure she's all right. I'll walk along the shore slowly... just tell me which way. But you need to go to her, okay?" When he didn't answer, I pinched his shoulder. "*Okay?*"

"Okay."

"I'm not about to fall for another trap, Sahcor."

He nodded, though we knew that wasn't the only danger here. Before either of us could change our minds, Sahcor drew me to him, and I pulled myself against his back to wrap my arms around his neck. A burst of speed had the seawater splashing over my face, and I had to close my eyes against the onslaught and the cool wind. After a short while, Sahcor straightened, and when I released my hold on him, my feet hit the sand under the water. He waited until I had splashed to shore, and after he pointed to his left, I nodded and began moving in that direction.

I watched as he dived under the water and disappeared, left alone with my thoughts about what I should do.

CHAPTER 28

MISHA

Ultimately, I figured the best way to think through this was to put myself in the other girls' shoes. If a Synth showed up, I would have a million questions for them, wondering if they knew where my friends were and if they were safe.

I didn't know much about the girls I was taken with, but I'm certain they would try to look for me.

And the only way to stop them was to tell them myself.

If I explained, *surely* they would understand. If they knew I was safe now, and I insisted they leave me alone, would they do it? It was better than leaving them in the dark because if they *didn't* know, they might never stop looking, and I didn't want that either. They needed to know I was okay so they could go back to wherever they were on this continent, far away from the Ghaal colony.

It wasn't long before I came across Sahcor, standing on the beach, facing off with one of the girls—Tori, judging by her hair color, but while I remember it being long and straight, it was short and wild. She was with who I could only assume was another Synth, green and covered in vines as if he were made of the forest floor.

Adaptive, remember?

As I approached, Sahcor growled out, "There are *others.*"

"What do you mean?" Tori was yelling, and Sahcor's shoulders sagged. The weight of what we had been through, what he still held himself responsible for, and the knowledge we held was a lot. A whirlwind of thoughts passed through my mind, and I was *glad* Tori was here. Not because I had changed my mind but because it was so clear to me now—I'd picked up how headstrong she was even from our limited interactions. She and the others deserved to know I was okay, so they could leave me alone, guilt-free.

"He means..." Tori whipped around to face me, and her jaw dropped as I continued calmly, "Other than the four of us, there are other girls. The Ghaal have them. I've seen them."

Tori broke away from the Synth, who'd had his arms wrapped around her and moved toward me, crushing me against her chest in a tight hug. "Misha, thank fuck you're okay."

The hug was nice, for a moment, before my mind started counting how many humans were now within close proximity or already in the Ghaal's hands.

Four—me, Tori, and the two in stasis.

Tori needed to leave. I couldn't let myself get swept in any emotions during this moment. The green Synth watched my face carefully, and he must have picked up the vibes I was letting off as he snatched Tori's arm and pulled her against him again, a low growl rumbling through his chest. A sense of relief came over me. I liked that Tori had found a Synth to look after her.

I hoped the others had too.

"Something is wrong," the Synth said simply. He took a step away from me and dragged Tori with him.

"I'm safe, Tori..." I said, pleading with my eyes for her to understand. "But you shouldn't have come for me."

"How could I not?" Tori cried out. Desperately, she turned to look at the green Synth. "Vitri?" When he said nothing, she glanced between him and Sahcor, then to me, her brows drawing together.

"Can someone please tell me what the fuck is going on?"

Before I could answer, a powerful spasm shot through my body.

As though the Ghaal were right next to me with the weapon they'd used while in the cell, the shock was harsh and instant, rippling through my body for several moments before stopping as quickly as it started. The echo of the pain radiated through me. I dropped to my knees and cried out.

Sahcor rushed to my side as Tori called my name. "What's wrong?" Sahcor asked, brushing hair from my face.

A sob raked through my body as my back jerked again, a muscle spasm as an aftershock from the intensity of the pain. Staring at my arm where the Ghaal implant was, a light flashed intermittently, the deep orange blinking on and off.

Eyes wide, I lifted my head to Sahcor, my gaze flickering to Tori briefly. "I think they know she's here," I whispered urgently. Forcing myself to my feet, my legs shaking, I looked at Tori.

She needed an explanation.

But she also needed to get the fuck out of here.

"The Ghaal tagged me, Tori. I can't stay near you. They'll use me to find you. I'm sorry, you need to go." I took several steps away from her, shaking my head. "I'm okay, but please leave and don't follow me."

Turning on my heel, I sprinted down the beach, ignoring the sting of tears in my eyes as Tori screamed out my name.

I didn't stop.

I needed to get back to Sahcor's. We had to gather our supplies and leave *now*. Was the implant designed only to recognize when other humans were around? Or was it a tracker too?

Skidding to a halt, the sand sprayed up and stuck to my still-damp calves.

No. I couldn't go back to Sahcor's. Then they would know where he lived.

Glancing at the implant, it had stopped flashing.

Maybe it was only activated when I was close to another human.

Pressing the balls of my palms against my eyes, I sighed. There was too much guesswork here, and it's not like we could stroll into the Ghaal colony and ask them the parameters of the damn thing. I could have asked Sol, but I foolishly believed what they'd told me about its purpose.

Fuck.

"Fuck!" I shouted.

Turning when footsteps pounded behind me, my shoulders slumped when I saw Sahcor. Every ounce of energy I had drained from me at that moment, and when I collapsed to my knees again, Sahcor was right there with me, wrapped his arms around me, and held me as I sobbed against his chest.

"I don't know what to do," I cried, not even sure if I wanted to push him away or pull him closer. I opted to wrap my arms around him as he held me and curled my fingers to grip his shoulders. "I just don't know what to do. If I return to your home, the Ghaal will find me, and then I'm putting *you* in danger. If I run, they'll find me anyway. If I stay near the girls, then I'm putting them in danger." Pulling back, I met Sahcor's sad gaze. "Just tell me what to do. I don't know. *I don't know.*"

Sahcor said nothing, simply rocking gently as I started crying again. He held me until I couldn't cry anymore, and the breeze off the ocean had dropped a few degrees, although I'm not sure that was the reason I was shivering.

When I looked up, Sahcor was staring into the distance.

"What do you see?" I whispered, my throat dry.

"Nothing."

"What do you mean, *nothing?*"

When Sahcor looked at me, his expression was clear, back in that place in his mind where he figures things out, where he overthinks as much as I do. "No Ghaal."

"Just because you don't see anything doesn't mean they're not coming for me! It doesn't mean *this...*" I slapped my arm angrily and winced when the wound stung, "... isn't a tracker of some sort, set to go off when I get too close to the other girls."

"Oh, I'm certain it was set to go off when you were in the vicinity of the other human females, but you're not anymore."

"Wha—"

"It stopped flashing."

"I know that!" I ran my fingers through my hair, gripping and pulling as I stared at Sahcor. "Please. *Please* tell me what you're thinking because I think I'm going crazy and really need you to talk to me."

Sahcor's head snapped to me as if he just realized I was there, breaking him of whatever his thoughts were as I clung to him as my literal lifeline.

"I'm thinking we need to test if that is indeed a tracker or if it only works if you're in the vicinity of the other females."

"I'm *not* putting Tori in danger."

Sahcor's expression broke then, and he brushed his fingers down my cheek, humming as I tilted into his touch. His voice was softer as he said, "I'd never suggest you should, my mate." I sighed, releasing only a small amount of the tension in my chest. "I'm saying let's find a spot to hide, set up some traps, and see if the Ghaal come. If they don't, we'll return to my cave, gather our supplies, and leave."

"Together."

It wasn't a question, but Sahcor answered it anyway, "Yes." And he kissed the top of my head.

I needed him, probably more than he needed me. But I loved this being I clung to now, and hearing his heart beat gently as my ear pressed against his chest, a calm rhythm that pulled the rest of me into sync with him, I knew I didn't want to be without him. We'd do as he suggested, and I was thankful he could think clearly enough to have a plan. It made sense as I calmed. Why would they track me when I was alone? There was no point in getting only me—the Ghaal wanted us all together.

This wasn't over, but I was safe here, wrapped in Sahcor's arms. No matter where I was, I'd be safe with him and fight to protect him as much as he would me.

"I love you, Sahcor." I sighed, pressing my face against him and rubbing my cheek against his chest, wanting to be covered in his delicious scent.

"I love you, too, my mate."

EPILOGUE

SAHCOR

The supplies were packed, but my Misha wasn't happy.

"What's bothering you, my mate?" I asked.

She huffed out a laugh, her smile sad when she turned to me. "I just... *really* want to get rid of this implant. I'm so scared it's going to be a danger to you... to us."

I approached her, my footsteps echoing off the cave walls. "We waited all night, didn't we? The Ghaal never came for you."

"I guess..."

Watching her unspoken emotions move across

her face for a moment, I reached out and pulled her against me. "We'll find a way."

"Surely, the Ghaal have a tool or something? Something that can remove it?"

Snarling, I held her tighter. "You can't ask me to risk your safety."

Misha sighed. "I know, I'm sorry. I shouldn't have even suggested it."

The way her lips twisted as the thoughts passed through her mind made my chest ache, and I dropped the bag I'd been holding and kneeled in front of Misha. "What can I do to make you happy?"

The twist of her lips turned into a smile when her eyes settled on mine. *"You* make me happy."

"But you're not. I can see it in your eyes."

Her shoulders heaved as she sighed and lifted a hand to twirl my hair around her fingers. "I just still worry, you know? I can't get the Ghaal out of my head and cannot stop worrying that I'm putting you in danger. I want to be with you, I really do, but will I ever be able to rest if I think my presence makes everywhere I go unsafe for you?" Her eyes glazed over. "How could I forgive myself if something happened to you?"

"You're safe with me, Misha."

"I know I am." Her small palms cupped my cheeks, and as she kissed my lips, her bottom lip trembled. "But are you safe with me?"

"I have an idea."

"Okay…"

"One more night."

Her brows pulled together. "You're going to have to elaborate." I didn't miss the tug on her lip, almost a smirk.

"We'll stay here another night to see if the Ghaal come for us. We'll be ready if they do. But if they don't…" I grabbed her hands in mine, pressed my lips gently to the inside of her palm, and relished the way she relaxed into my touch. "You put this out of your head and simply focus on us together."

Her lips met mine in a rush, tears streaming down her cheeks as she still fought with indecision and guilt—things I couldn't take away but hopefully, in time, would ease. And I would be there for her, no matter what. Misha parted her lips and welcomed my tongue into her mouth, moaning as I moved forward and laid her underneath me. "Fuck me, Sahcor," she whispered and laced her fingers through my hair again. "Fuck me until I forget everything but you."

Her thighs parted, and the loincloth I'd made for travel was already pushed to the side as my cock hardened. Her cunt was already wet for me, and I shifted my hips until the head of my cock hit her clit, making her moan again before I drove into her.

"Misha…" I waited for her to open her eyes, to hold my gaze as I thrust my cock into her again and again and slowed down my thrusts to relish in the feel of her body under mine and her cunt as it squeezed me tight. "Look at me."

Her green eyes met mine, saying everything she couldn't find the words for and more.

"You're safe with me."

"Safe with you," she repeated. The stress in her eyes dissipated, even as the sheen of tears remained. "I love you."

"I love you too." The growling started in my chest as my hips snapped, pressing deeper into her. When she moaned, I swallowed the sound, thrusting faster until I couldn't even maintain the kiss any longer, and our lips simply hovered over each other's, sharing breaths as we both came to our highs.

"Gonna come..." she panted, clenching around me.

"Come for me, my mate."

When she came, she pushed me over the edge, too, and I groaned, my voice echoing around the cave as I fucked Misha through her orgasm and filled her with my cum.

We stayed like that for a long while, with my forehead pressed to hers as we came down. I tucked my arms under her shoulders and held her close, never wanting to let her go again. Where our abdomens met, I imagined the day I would feel a pulse under her skin, a tiny heartbeat of the life that would be our child. I stilled on top of her, straining my senses, but there wasn't a response.

Not yet. It would be too soon to tell anyway.

Misha spoke before I could tell her my thoughts. "Are you happy?" she whispered.

My chest tightened. "Very happy."

"Don't you miss your brothers?"

"Of course I do. I always have. This life of solitude isn't easy."

"It must be hard." She sighed, stretching her neck to kiss my chin. "But it's not solitude anymore. You have me, and I have you, don't I?"

"Always."

Continue with...
Releaser – Elements of Abduction Book 5
for
Amy and Eldich's story

Amy wakes after years in stasis in captivity.
An alien promises her freedom, but every second
he spends trying to rescue her puts him in danger,
and Amy doesn't want her freedom to come at the
cost of his life.

ACKNOWLEDGMENTS

Thank you to my super fans who keep me going and to all those I can have ridiculous conversations about fucking aliens with.

ANGELS AND FIRE BOOKS

Find our exciting stories at:
www.angelsandfirebooks.com.au

READER GROUP

Want access to fun, prizes and sneak peeks?
Join my Facebook Reader Group.
https://www.facebook.com/groups/588038442170571

Liberator

NEWSLETTER
Sign up for my Newsletter.
https://www.subscribepagye.com/angelsandfirebooks

BOOKBUB
https://www.bookbub.com/authors/stefanie-dawn

GOODREADS
Add my books to your TBR list
on my Goodreads profile.
https://www.goodreads.com/author/
show/21761217.Stefanie_Dawn

AMAZON
https://www.amazon.com/author/stefaniedawn

WEBSITE
http://www.angelsandfirebooks.com.au/

INSTAGRAM
https://www.instagram.com/angelsandfirebooks

EMAIL
info@angelsandfirebooks.com.au

FACEBOOK
https://www.facebook.com/stefaniedawnwriter

ABOUT THE AUTHOR

Stefanie Dawn has been a writer and creative soul all her life **and** strives to give her readers stories they can escape into as they become absorbed in the worlds created.

When she isn't writing, Stefanie might be painting, reading, or watching movies. She loves the process of producing films as another form of storytelling. There's also a good chance she'll be baking some delicious treats—pretending she won't later regret consuming them—or simply enjoying a cocktail with friends.

Stefanie Dawn lives in South Australia with her ever-supportive partner and a lovable gang of rescue cats.

You can stay up to date with
Stefanie and her books at:
www.angelsandfirebooks.com.au